A TANZIE LEWIS NOVEL

REVENGE

— *of the* —

CUBE

DWELLER

JOANNE FOX PHILLIPS

RIVER GROVE
BOOKS

D0974406

Published by River Grove Books
Austin, TX
www.rivergrovebooks.com

Distributed by River Grove Books

For ordering information or special discounts for bulk purchases, please contact River Grove Books at PO Box 91869, Austin, TX 78709, 512.891.6100.

Design and composition by Greenleaf Book Group
Cover design by Greenleaf Book Group

Cover images:
©iStockphoto.com/Jaymast
©shutterstock.com/Geo Martinez

Publisher's Cataloging-In-Publication Data

Phillips, Joanne Fox, 1958-
Revenge of the cube dweller / Joanne Fox Phillips.—First edition.

    pages : illustration ; cm.—(A Tanzie Lewis novel)

Issued also as an ebook.
ISBN: 978-1-938416-93-4

    1. Auditors—Oklahoma—Tulsa—Fiction. 2. Fraud investigation—Oklahoma—Tulsa—Fiction. 3. Corporations—Corrupt practices—Oklahoma—Tulsa—Fiction. 4. Women in the professions—Oklahoma—Tulsa—Fiction. 5. Revenge—Fiction. 6. Suspense fiction. I. Title.

PS3616.H555 R48 2014
813/.6   2014935832

First Edition

Other Edition(s)
eBook ISBN: 978-1-938416-94-1

For Clayton, Ted, and Phil
And for my brother Charlie, who inspired
the storyteller in all of his sisters

CHAPTER ONE

Around seven o'clock on Easter Sunday morning, I pull my black Lexus into a narrow parking spot in the garage. Usually I worry about getting dinged by the pickup trucks with the spaces so close together, but by timing my visit on the holiday that is unlikely. With no other vehicles in the garage, it is as I've planned—no one is here to interfere.

The manila folder with the building schematic printout had slid off the passenger seat onto the floor during the drive over from my condo. I gather the papers, straightening them with a tap on the top of my thigh, and tuck them under my arm as I get out of the car and walk across the street. The absence of traffic somehow makes the building feel even more ominous than usual.

The angry presence of the giant thirty-story black granite tower looks out of place on the Tulsa skyline among its neighbors, charming art deco buildings erected during the 1920s when Oklahoma's second-largest city was the oil capital of the world. Tulsans are proud of their modern and their vintage architecture, but opinions have always been mixed about the Bishop building, which stands out because of its color, size, and total lack of architectural distinction.

Through the smoky glass at the north entrance, I see no one manning the guard desk. A key card is required both to enter the building and to access the elevator bank, so I push the intercom button next to the revolving door and wait. A scratchy voice asks me what I want.

"I'm a Bishop Group employee," I say, "but I've forgotten my key card." I have planned what I will say next if the voice asks me any questions and have a false identity at the ready to test how far I can get without proper credentials, but I don't even get the chance to use it.

"Okay, I'll buzz you in," the voice says. There is a loud clack indicating that the lock on the main glass door to the building has been released.

"Hey wait," I call into the intercom. "I need to get to my floor. Can someone help me out?"

"Okay," says the voice from the speaker box, "I'll send security."

I take advantage of the unlocked door and wait inside. To pass the time, I look at the enormous murals adorning the lobby. They show the taming of Oklahoma: cowboys, oil gushers, and covered wagons with families. *Really horrible art*, I think to myself, and I wonder who they gave the commission to—probably a Bishop family member.

I open my folder on the counter of the empty guard station and review the blueprints one last time. Having gained access to the building, I plan to check out the security protocol for the second level of impregnability—the automated panels that part like a subway gate and lead to the elevators when a valid security badge is swiped through the card reader. Any unauthorized person who can make it as far as the elevators will be able to access all but the executive floors, which require additional clearance. Once in, an intruder might be able to steal unsecured laptops containing sensitive information or create other problems for a controversial company like Bishop. My objective today is to see what and how much I can expect to get away with.

After a while, a blond security guard emerges from the stairwell and approaches me. He looks to be all of eighteen years old and has a single iPod earbud wire connecting his left ear to the breast pocket of a poorly fitting blue blazer with "Keith" inscribed on the plastic nameplate. Even at a distance I can detect the ferocious bass of rap music that will no doubt render him deaf by his thirtieth birthday.

"Hi," I say walking toward him. "I forgot my badge and I need to get to my office."

I'm careful not to say my name, and I'm pretty surprised when Keith swipes his card and follows me past the now-open Plexiglas barriers to the elevator bank. I wait for him to ask me for some sort of ID, but he doesn't.

"Are you good, or do you need to get to an executive floor?" asks Keith.

I am caught off guard by the question. Maybe it is my Gucci loafers or the diamond tennis bracelet, or just that all middle-aged women look like executive material to a kid, but I feel flattered nonetheless. In my original plan, I never contemplated gaining access to the executive floors.

"Why yes," I say, seizing the opportunity before thinking about it. "Thanks. Thirty, please."

I'm going for broke here. The executive floors, twenty-five through thirty, require a third level of security and can be accessed only by a select few, including security—and, for today at least, me.

Keith flashes his card over the tiny red light and the top button illuminates. We ride up together without conversation. He seems as bored as a five-year-old at the opera, and I sense he is anxious to get back to what he was doing before I showed up. Still, I feel a brief bond when I look down and notice my right foot and his tapping to the backbeat of a Lil Wayne partying song I had heard in a Zumba class a few months back.

When we exit the elevator, Keith stands next to me as if waiting for me to give him directions. If he were doing his job properly, he'd stay with me while I'm on the floor to keep an eye on what I'm doing, but I don't think Keith is too clear about what he is supposed to do.

I take a chance. "You know, I have my office key. I don't need you to let me in."

He looks relieved. "Oh, all right then." He steps back into the elevator. "Have a nice day," he says. I watch the elevator door close and Keith disappear. Just like that, I have penetrated the mighty Bishop Group's inner sanctum.

Looking around the thirtieth floor, I am astonished to find that the doors to all the executive offices are wide open. I had assumed they would be locked and had thought about asking Keith to let me into one of them. Turns out I didn't need to. I'm uncertain whether the doors have been left open by the cleaning crew or just not locked in the first place, but I delight in the free and open access. Who knows what I might find if I rummage around?

The overhead lights are not on, but enough morning sun leaks through the open office doors for me to see my way around. Enormous bookshelves filled with expensive doodads and awards flank the elevator doors, and a fabulous antique Louis XV sideboard, bigger than most dining room tables, serves as the reception desk. The absence of the usual hums, buzzes, and beeps of normal office activity makes me aware of my own footsteps as I poke around the main area, testing locked drawers and cabinets and checking out the wastebaskets for confidential discards.

Roaming through the hallways reminds me of when, in another time and another place, I would meet my then-husband Winston for lunch or after hours to attend a corporate event. I didn't need to sneak onto the executive floor then. "Oh hello, Mrs. Lewis," they would say. "It's so good to see you again. Can I get you something? Coffee? A soda?"

I have never been to *this* executive floor before. Peons like me are relegated to cube farms on floors with single digits. Still, the lay of the land is typical and easy to figure out. Most building plans follow the same basic formula. Corner offices outrank the other window offices, and relative square footage is based on hierarchy. Baldwin Bishop's office is in the northwest corner and consumes about 20 percent of the thirtieth floor. There is no nameplate on the door or wall, but I know it's his office just from the rich walnut paneling surrounding the entryway that I have read about previously in a *Tulsa World* article. The wood was salvaged from a castle in Wales and imported specifically for Baldwin's area.

A small vestibule where his assistant Marla stands sentry during the week is, of course, unattended, and I sit down at her meticulously organized desk to collect my thoughts and figure out what I should do next. As I sit there, I wonder if I have already gone too far by not just riding down with Keith once I'd gained access. But I may never again get the opportunity to snoop around like this. Although the office doors are open, Marla's desk is locked, so I snoop where I can, hitting pay dirt almost immediately.

In an effort to bolster IT security, passwords increasingly require more and more complicated syntax and also need to be changed every ninety days. No longer could someone's password simply be "password" and remain constant throughout his or her career. Further, each program has different requirements so that a single password will not work for every application. While the intention was to increase security, the result has been quite the opposite.

For the average employee, there is no practical way to keep track of the constantly changing passwords other than writing them down somewhere. The usual choices are a sticky note affixed to the underside of the keyboard, a notepad kept in the top right desk drawer, or a piece of paper pinned to the bulletin board next to the monitor. Marla, being as old and forgetful as I am, keeps her list underneath a lovely pen set given her by Baldwin to commemorate twenty-five years of devoted service.

I make note of Marla's passwords on my iPhone. Her user ID follows the same convention as all other Bishop employees. MWALTERS, I type into the login screen of her computer, along with the password GOJayhawks!17. *Access denied* flashes back at me: *incorrect user ID or password.* I try the next password on her list: Divalady$18. And with that, I am in.

I access her Microsoft Outlook account and think about sending a rude e-mail just for grins, but instead I scan her inbox and her sent files. From the volume of e-mail, it appears that Marla is routinely copied on Baldwin Bishop's correspondence, probably so she can organize it into folders and protect it from the auto-purge that occurs on a rolling ninety-day interval.

A particular subject chain that piques my interest involves potential layoffs if Bishop's maritime sector doesn't start to improve. I read further into it. Baldwin blames the sour economy, but the consulting firm blames the inexperience of the business unit president, who as it turns out is Baldwin's nephew Brandon. There are some e-mails about possibly moving Brandon into something else and letting one of the "go-getters" take over the reins for a while until maritime gets back on its feet. I cannot imagine the delicate balance required to successfully manage a conglomerate while protecting the egos of family members.

There is other correspondence from Building Services saying that to cut costs, Starbucks coffee will no longer be served in the coffee bars below the twenty-fifth floor. A generic brand, Best Java, will be substituted, and it is estimated that the cost savings will be over $50,000 a year.

Bummer. The nephew of a bigwig screws up and now the little guy has to drink bad coffee. Isn't that how it always goes?

In addition to the Outlook account, Marla has a number of secured folders on her desktop that look interesting to me. I glance at my watch, though, and start to get nervous. As entertaining as it is to read all the juicy executive correspondence, I decide not to press my luck by hanging around.

I fish a flash drive out of my purse and plug it into the USB port on Marla's desktop. In less than five minutes, I transfer about six or seven folders from Marla's shared drive and restricted access folders. I don't know what they contain, but they are labeled, LEAR, ENV, and other acronyms I can decipher at a later time. I make a quick sweep of Baldwin's office, but his desk is locked, and I cannot find his password list as easily as Marla's.

Baldwin's office could double for a museum with all the sports memorabilia he has displayed. A signed Joe Montana Kansas City Chiefs jersey is mounted next to a baby blue George Brett one from the Royals, which in turn is hanging next to a yellow Wilt Chamberlain jersey from the Lakers. Another seven or eight jerseys hang next to those three. Photographs of Baldwin with various athletic stars blanket the other wall and eclipse the beautiful imported walnut paneling underneath. I envision a Welsh nobleman rolling over in his grave.

Baldwin's desk is not Louis XV like the sideboard; instead, it's a massive, manly, walnut monstrosity that is clearly expensive but not attractive, in my opinion. Not that it matters, since all the smaller sports paraphernalia crowds the surface area around his computer.

Autographed basketballs encapsulated in Plexiglas cubes from forty years' worth of University of Kansas teams consume his entire bookshelf and spill over to the credenza behind his desk. Smaller transparent cubes with autographed baseballs and footballs are stacked on top of the basketballs, and the couple of framed photos of what look like Baldwin's wife, children, and grandchildren are perched like afterthoughts atop the mementos. To me, this reeks of hoarding on a higher economic scale than old newspapers and garbage.

In one of the corners stands a commercial-sized elliptical machine and weight rack, and next to them is a door that leads to a lovely private bath with a shower and sauna. There is an adjoining closet that I poke my head into that has some emergency suits, shirts, ties, shoes, and some drawers presumably for underwear and socks.

I can't resist and slide the medicine cabinet door open, revealing only some Lipitor and an expired bottle of Tylenol. No hidden drug problem for this guy—no condoms or Viagra in case he wants to get frisky with Marla; only a well-worn Bible lying on a small table by the toilet. As I leave, I wonder exactly which verse would be appropriate inspiration for a bowel movement.

I glance at my watch again, mouthing a silent expletive as I gather my belongings and head back to the elevator. Once in the lobby, I realize that I need a card to get through the Plexiglas security gate, so I press the help button on my side of the partition and wait once again for Keith. In my younger days I could have climbed over the gate easily, but I am fifty-two now, and I don't think I can do it at this stage of the game. "Get what you needed?" Keith asks as he swipes his card, allowing me to pass through.

"Yeah, thanks."

"Well, you have a happy Easter, ma'am," Keith says, smiles, and walks over to the main exit with me, strutting to the rhythm of some horrific urban diatribe.

"You too," I say and I wave back as I cross the street over to the employee garage.

Sitting in my car, I reflect on what I just did. My boss in Internal

Audit had asked me to test building security, but as with most of my endeavors I have let my enthusiastic curiosity get the better of me and crossed a line that could get me fired. And all I have to show for it is a USB drive full of files with acronyms I don't understand—at least, not yet.

CHAPTER TWO

My name is Tanzie Lewis and I am an internal auditor for the Bishop Group.

When I first snagged my job interview, I did a little research that gave me some background info on the company and on the Bishop brothers. The Bishop Group, the ninth-largest private company in the United States in 2010, was founded by two brothers, Baldwin and Bennet Bishop, whose shrewd business know-how turned a sizable inheritance into a world-class fortune. Both boys had been standouts on the University of Kansas basketball team and had donated the funds to build and name the Bishop Basketball Pavilion on the KU campus in the early '90s.

Based on their appearance now as older men, it always strikes me as a little odd that the Bishops were once so athletic. Yes, they are both tall—six foot four or so—with Bennet being slightly taller than Baldwin. However, their narrow shoulders and wide hips make them unusually shaped for men in general and male athletes in particular. They are pear shaped, like the Country Bear Jamboree characters I once saw at Disneyland. There clearly is a dominant gene in play; with such a distinctive silhouette, you can easily spot a Bishop family member anywhere in the company.

Bennet is the Chief Executive Officer and Baldwin the Chief Operating Officer. The division seems to work well, and from what I had read, there is little to no rivalry or tension between the brothers. They think alike on most matters, and share a common passion for amassing an empire that will wield significant conservative influence for generations to come.

Bishop Group is diversified and includes agriculture, textiles, and maritime segments, but the largest and most profitable is their midstream oil and gas operation. Midstream represents the activity sandwiched between drilling for oil and selling the gas you put in a car. It includes pipelines that move the product from the wells to the refineries, big tanks that store the oil until there is room in the pipeline, and gas-processing plants that extract liquids such as the propane used in the family barbeque. It is not glamorous, but it can be hugely profitable.

My ex-husband Winston's company was in upstream, or exploration and production—the sexy part of the "bidness," as insiders refer to it. Upstream attracts gamblers, risk takers who go big and make huge fortunes off a gusher or go broke on a dry hole. Sometime in the early '90s the major oil companies shed their midstream assets because their returns were far less than the upstream and downstream activity could generate. This was when the Bishop boys entered the midstream business, buying whatever they could. The unglamorous but steady returns played perfectly into their Middle American sensibilities, just like marrying the girl from church rather than following in J. Howard Marshall's footsteps with Anna Nicole Smith.

Since Bishop is a privately held company, having an internal audit function is not a requirement like it is for companies traded on the New York Stock Exchange. But rumor had it that Bennet and Baldwin Bishop wanted to demonstrate a proactive approach to corporate governance, which is why in 2010 they tapped my boss, Hal Webber, to put an Internal Audit department together.

Water cooler gossip gave me the lowdown on Hal's history when I first settled in at Bishop. Back in the late '70s, he had been a second-string lineman for the University of Oklahoma football team and an honors graduate in the challenging field of mechanical engineering. He was the total package, as they say, and he'd had his pick of opportunities when he graduated. Hal married his college sweetheart and built up his career working in various operations arms of the Oklahoma energy industry.

If he had not pursued a career at Bishop, Hal could have easily succeeded in politics. He remembers names and emits a friendly, backslapping aura that makes him beloved in the organization. Everyone I've been in contact with at Bishop seems to think of Hal as a great guy. As far as heartland Tea Party values are concerned, Hal is as good as it gets. He goes to church every Sunday with his wife, Nancy, at the South Tulsa Baptist church, volunteers with the pro-life society of Oklahoma, and carries a concealed weapon in case he needs to intervene in a mass shooting or robbery.

Hal prides himself on staying in top physical form and has to special order his shirts to accommodate a neck bigger than the trunks of the scrub oaks lining the Arkansas River. From the looks of it, Hal deals with his receding hairline by shaving his head completely and sporting one of those '90s style goatees to compensate for his lack of treetop foliage. Bishop has a business casual dress code, but Hal always wears a suit and tie with an OU pin on his jacket lapel to project an image of importance consistent with his high regard for himself.

Hal is great with people and numbers, so when he was given authority over the gas-processing division in the late '90s, there had been little doubt he could handle the responsibility. He brought in tons of business and was considered a key contributor to Bishop's growing dominance in the midstream arena. But although Hal brought in producers, he was inexperienced in contract negotiations and did not fully understand the complexities of gas profitability dynamics. Unfortunately, this critical flaw allowed sharper cookies in the world of gas marketing to include clauses that protected, at Bishop's expense, their interests in cases of commodity price downturns.

After the crash in 2008, natural gas prices plummeted the following year, resulting not only in tens of millions of dollars' worth of losses but also the exposure of the disadvantageous contract terms that had been written under Hal's watch. It is not uncommon in the world of business to have seemingly brilliant careers derailed when incompetence surfaces during an economic hiccup. Ruthless as they supposedly are, however, even the Bishop brothers did not have the heart to fire Hal. As in the case of many chief auditors before him, the job was created as a way to administer palatable punishment.

It seems Hal is still beloved in the organization, but it's also clear the executive team no longer considers him an integral player. Hal copes with his demotion by inflating the status of his new position as Bishop's Vice President of Internal Audit as one of the most important jobs in the company. He brags to anyone who will listen that he was handpicked to oversee this critical function and assemble the new crack team. Still, it is clear to those who pay attention that he doesn't participate in the Monday morning executive sessions with Bennet and Baldwin, and his corner office on twenty-nine has been replaced by a much smaller one on six. Gone are his administrative assistant, Southern Hills golf membership, and access to the private plane fleet.

I used to be married to an oil and gas executive in Houston, and I have a deep understanding of the male ego and all the sad little things that men do to dissipate the sting of failure in the world of office politics. While Winston's failures were few and far between, I had a ringside seat to the real pain he felt because of his occasional business setbacks. I witnessed heavy drinking and sometimes found out that he'd had his wounds licked by some harlot, until he was able to gather himself, spin the story, and figure out a way to correct the career setback. Hal was no Winston, but the result was the same: In the end, he did everything he could to convince people that his demotion was actually a career advancement, a needed change, or a really exciting opportunity to broaden skills.

Hal probably thought about early retirement, but most likely his portfolio had tanked with the stock market crash and he just couldn't afford it. Besides, Hal would not be a quitter. No, he strikes me as the type of guy who would make hash browns out of horseshit, put his best smile on, and redeem himself in the eyes of the Bishop illuminati.

Hal told me how, after consulting with his new peers among the energy companies in Tulsa, he began putting this department together. He hired two managers: Moe, an operational auditor from a small midstream company in Kansas, and Frank, fresh out of Boyd and Associates, a second-tier CPA firm in Tulsa. I don't believe the chosen two are considered top talent, which is usually obtained from risk consulting firms or one of the larger companies in Oklahoma.

Certainly Bishop is an attractive place to work in Tulsa, and Hal could have easily had his pick from a very experienced pool of candidates from some of the companies shedding personnel during the economic belt-tightening going on then. Knowing Hal though, he probably could not bring himself to hire people who would make him look stupid by knowing more than he did. At that time, he was probably still red-assed about his fall from grace and wanted to make sure that some young whipper-snapper didn't take what little he had left by outshining him at a meeting with the big boys.

Hal hired me as a staff auditor in December 2009 to do the many necessary grunt tasks below the ego grade of my three superiors—Hal, Moe, and Frank. I graduated with honors from UC Berkeley with a degree in accounting and moved to Houston shortly afterward for purely economic reasons. In 1981 an oil boom was in full force, and outside of Anchorage, Alaska, Houston was paying the highest salaries in the nation for accountants. I figured I would work for a year, make some money, and then head back home to San Francisco. One year turned into two and then nine, and soon I was an oil and gas specialist pretty well chained to the energy industry.

I married an oil executive who allowed me to ditch my career and focus on more personal interests. Giving up my job was not difficult. Accounting, particularly in the public accounting firms, is intense stress within a bubble of mind-numbing tedium. I walked away grateful and happy, until I was "outplaced" by my husband in favor of a younger and thinner version of myself twenty years later. Before that I never thought I would utter the word "debit" or "credit" unless it was followed by "card."

The fresh start of Tulsa seemed like a good idea at the time; it is still within the energy corridor, but out of Texas and far away from the sting of rejection and the humiliation of having been discarded. Of course I'd known that entering the workforce again after such a long break wouldn't be a picnic.

"I can bring you on, but only at an entry-level," Hal told me at the end of our interview, "until you prove yourself. Look, Tanzie," Hal nodded sympathetically, "I understand how difficult it must be for a girl like you having to go back to work after so many years. My Nancy used to work the cash register at the Kmart before we got married. She's so friendly, you know. Everyone just loved her. I'm not sure what she'd do if something happened to me and she had to go back to work."

He placed a fatherly hand on my shoulder as he escorted me from his office.

I wasn't sure which was more shocking: Hal's complete disregard for human resources protocol or his comparison of me, a former financial consultant, to a cashier.

Based on that interview, I'm quite certain that Hal has no idea who he's hired. Under the pleading smile of a desperate, middle-aged woman content with scanning documents and fixing paper jams is the soul of a competitor. My plan is to remain patient and build a reputation for diligence, and I know the opportunities will eventually materialize.

If all goes as planned, in five years, I'll have a corner office somewhere at Bishop. I am smart and driven and have nothing to do other than work, which is a clear recipe for success. Today's audit, with the productive gumshoeing I did around the executive office, is proof that I am capable of going the extra mile to bring in results. Moe and Frank don't stand a chance against me—and neither will be smart enough to realize this before it's too late.

After finagling my way into the Bishop building, I arrive back at my condo at 8:45 a.m. On the way home I picked up a pack of Virginia Slims. Cigarettes are cheaper in Tulsa than in Houston and cheaper still when purchased from one of the Indian smoke shops that can sell them at reduced state tax rates. Typically, I smoke two cigarettes a day: one with my morning coffee and the second with an evening glass of white wine.

This is a secret I keep from just about everyone since there are such strong negative opinions about smokers. The Bishop building is smoke-free. For me to smoke at the office would be career suicide. Except for coffee drinking, the Bishop management team could pass for Mormon: no drinking, smoking, swearing, or skirt chasing. Winston's company was exactly the opposite; yet another example of the difference between upstream and midstream.

I pour a cup of coffee from the coffeemaker I'd set to brew at eight thirty, grab my portable landline, and open the sliding glass door to my tiny balcony that overlooks Utica Square, an upscale shopping center anchored by the smallest Saks Fifth Avenue in the United States. I didn't have my cigarette this morning because I left pretty early to get downtown. I light one up, take the first drag, and place it on the crystal ashtray I keep on a small table by my patio chair.

The view from my balcony is charming, with expanses of tulips and pansies bordering the empty parking lots. There is not a single person at the square this morning, only the bronze statues of children and a wooden chainsaw carving of a Victorian woman. All the real people are probably at church. Tulsa is religious, and Bishop is even more so. I have seen mostly white Christians, and devout ones at that, in the corridors of my workplace. During my six-month tenure, I have been invited no fewer than eleven times to join a fellow employee for a church service. Everyone knows I am new to Tulsa, which means I'm fresh meat for any congregation. It never crosses anyone's mind that I might not go to church.

I don't. I'm an alumna of the Catholic Church and parochial schools, and I've already heard enough Kyrie Eleison for a lifetime. My response to these invitations has always been the same. "That is so nice, but I am attending services with my new neighbor at"—I make something up to say here—"but I will let you know if I feel like venturing out." This is a pretty easy out because there are more churches in Tulsa than I have ever seen anywhere before.

My thoughts are shaken loose by the telephone ringing, and I pick it up and say, "Hello, Lucy."

My sister Lucy, while not a card-carrying eco-terrorist, is surely a sympathizer, and at first she was horrified that I was working for Bishop. It is well known that Bennet and Baldwin Bishop fund conservative think tanks determined to undermine the social progress made in the past fifty years. Furthermore, Bishop is infamous among environmentalists for being one of the worst polluters and is the target of many a Sierra Club exposé. But Lucy is a bleeding heart in all respects and understands that a fifty-year-old woman who's been out of the workforce for twenty years doesn't have many options and needs health insurance, if nothing else. I believe she was sad that I hadn't elected to take her up on her offer to move to her farm and live in the vintage airstream trailer she keeps for visitors, but even the biggest extremist can give way to rationalization when her sister is involved.

Lucy is extraordinarily well organized and schedules her calls like appointments. Every Sunday at 9:00 a.m. Tulsa time, I hear "Call from Lucy" announced by the caller ID. I refresh my coffee cup and hunker down for another episode of the latest adventures of Lucy O'Leary, organic farmer and sheep herder, and silently thank God I live in relative comfort, spared from castration duty or hand weeding acres of organic heirloom wheat.

"You bought a gun?" I ask. "You are the last person I would ever think of as owning a gun. Do you even know how to shoot one?"

"Well not a real gun, a paintball gun," Lucy replies. "I lost three lambs this week to those coyotes."

"Paintball?"

"I don't want to kill them, just to discourage them, get them to realize preying on my lambs comes with a blast of purple or yellow paint. I really think that over time this will curb their behavior."

"And just how long do you think it will take for the coyotes to make that connection? Are there clinical studies on behavior modification of coyotes? What if it backfires, Lucy? What if they actually think it's fashionable to have purple and yellow fur? Then what?"

"Ha ha ha, smartass! Want to borrow my gun and tag a Bishop brother or two? Perhaps we can modify *their* behavior," Lucy says.

"Oh, speaking of which," I say and tell her about getting onto the executive floor this morning.

"Too bad I didn't know this before. I might have asked you to drop off some Sierra Club literature."

"Anyway, his secretary leaves her passwords practically out in plain sight, so I downloaded some files."

Lucy immediately gets more serious. "What kind of files? What's in them?"

"Oh, I don't know," I say, nervous about her sudden interest. "I just got carried away. You know how I am. And besides, that's not the point. The point is that there is this perception that Bishop security is impenetrable, and I proved it's fairly easy to breach. They need to know that they have some pretty big holes that need to be filled."

"Oh, before I forget," Lucy says, changing the subject, "I spoke with Honey last night. Little Lulu got into NYU Tisch School of the Arts! Can you believe it? Broadway bound!" Lulu, our niece, is the youngest daughter of my third sister

Bumby. Honey, our eldest sister, the one who keeps us all connected, is a Catholic nun, and Bumby is the single mother of three daughters. Her husband Shamus was killed in a car wreck ten years ago.

"The tuition's upwards of $50,000 a year and NYU offers a little aid, but not much. Bumby wants to know if you can help with tuition like you did for the others."

"Yikes! Lucy. Does it make sense to drop a quarter of a million bucks on an education that could relegate her to waiting tables for the rest of her life?" I am stalling here, pondering the dismal returns I'm making on my portfolio these days. "I thought she wanted to be a nurse like her sisters."

"She's always wanted to act, she just didn't think she'd get in anywhere like NYU. This is a huge opportunity, Tanzie. They're very selective."

Winston and I had no children of our own and gladly helped the nieces and nephews pay for their education. Now that Winston has become my wasband, I am fairly certain he will not continue to fund the O'Leary scholarship program. Still, it will not hurt to ask; that kind of money can probably be found under a seat cushion in his home, considering his outrageous executive salary. Plus, he has always adored Lulu and Bumby.

The idea of getting in touch with Winston, however, makes me wince. Maybe I can do it without bothering him. Fifty thousand a year will put a big dent in my portfolio, but I'm not going to be a grunt forever. In a couple of years, I might be making well over six figures a year. I'm not going to let my adorable Lulu turn down a chance like this.

"Of course I will," I finally say. "Tell her not to worry. We can figure something out. Find out from Bumby when she needs the money, okay?"

"Okay, I will."

In our family, we often communicate indirectly, particularly when favors are asked. That way, the requester will not be humiliated if the request is denied. I don't know if this is a European thing or just an O'Leary thing, but that's how our business is taken care of. Lucy and I end our call with our family's traditional Greek Easter greeting that we've repeated every Easter since childhood.

"Christos Anesti," Lucy says.

"Alithos Anesti," I reply as I hang up.

After my chat, I type up my notes from the morning's security review and go back over them in preparation for the next day's staff meeting. I smile and nod. This is my ticket. The simple request to validate base-level building security, thanks to me, has revealed breaches so profound that if the wrong people decided to take advantage of them, they could potentially bring down the company. The competitor in me cannot wait to see Moe and Frank react when I deliver my report. This is first-class work and perhaps the vehicle to move me out from under Moe and Frank altogether and into an office beside them.

CHAPTER THREE

take extra time getting ready this morning in preparation for the big meeting, applying root touchup to the hint of gray emerging from where my hair parts and selecting the perfect outfit. The expensive black knit St. John suit is a good choice because it screams money, power, and good taste. Most important, though, the stretchy material enables the wearer to look great anywhere within a four-size range.

"Hi there, girlie, you're lookin' pretty today." It's just before 9:00 a.m. Monday morning. I have been at my desk a full two hours before Hal gets to work. With a "World's Best Dad" coffee mug in one hand and his briefcase in the other, he leans against my cube opening and waits for me to turn around and reciprocate the greeting.

"Did you have a nice Easter, Hal?"

"Yes I did, Tanzie, yes I did. We all went to church, of course.

Then we had everyone over for lunch and the Webber Annual Egg Hunt. Little Mike won again this year; that's three in a row."

I smile politely at my boss and listen attentively as he continues the blow-by-blow coverage. Engineers tend to be even more detail oriented than accountants, so Hal's descriptions leave nothing out: what everyone wore, what was in each Easter basket, and what was served for lunch.

"Nancy baked a ham and made one of those casseroles, what are they called—with the green beans, onions, and canned soup?"

"Green bean casserole?"

"Oh yes, that's it! That's it. Green bean casserole. You girls sure understand a way to a man's heart. And pie. No restaurant can make a crust like Nancy. Don't ask her to balance a checkbook, though. Girls have so much trouble with math. Don't know why; maybe God just made them that way." Hal leans down toward me. "And I'm glad he did," he whispers.

"I have a CPA, Hal. I can balance a checkbook," I say and smile.

"Whoa, now, miss women's lib. SORRY!" He backs away, waving his hands in exaggerated regret. "I forgot you're from California. I meant most girls." Hal chuckles. "Some girls, like you, Tanzie, are great with numbers. Very good trench workers."

"Thanks, Hal. I appreciate the compliment. Do you think—"

"Keep dressing up like today, Tanzie, and it won't be long before you find a new husband and can quit this job."

I let out a sigh as I sit back down and watch Hal walk toward his office. I look at my clock. I have about five minutes before the staff meeting, so I visit the ladies' room for a fresh coat of lipstick and a quick quality check for lint or stray hairs. I take some deep breaths and rehearse in my head exactly how I am going to present my findings.

There are only four of us, so we fit around Hal's small table rather than tie up a conference room. I am the lowest on the totem pole, but I report directly to Hal. That is a political move, because he has two managers and doesn't want to upset either of them with a disproportionate reporting structure. Thus, even though both Moe and Frank assign my work, and I have only limited contact with Hal, I am invited to the Monday morning roundtable.

The meeting begins with an update of what is on Hal's calendar that week: meetings, business trips, and lunches with important people. Then he goes around the room asking Moe and Frank to let him know what they are working on and about any progress that has been made since the last meeting. Generally, I don't have a speaking part, and Frank and Moe answer for me because I work under their supervision. Frank begins his update using the checklist on the memo pad he uses to keep track of his reportable events. I watch him tick the little boxes he has drawn beside each item as he goes down the list.

The most noteworthy thing about Frank is that he is not noteworthy. He is completely ordinary in every respect: neither handsome nor homely; he smiles infrequently and laughs even less; he is medium height, medium weight, about thirty years old with a blond number-three buzz cut. Eyewitness descriptions, should he venture into a life of crime, would narrow the field to about every third man in Tulsa. If not for the cheap polyester ties he favors, Frank would blend in with any beige wall in the Bishop building.

———◆———

My second day on the job, Frank asked me to review some reports for him and give input. Trained in the old-fashioned way of Big Eight public accounting firms, I went through the report footing the columns and making sure everything was tip-top. As Frank walked by my cube, I asked him, "Do you want me to make a list of the errors I find and discuss them all at once, or go over each report separately?" I was pretty sure Frank was testing me to see if I could help with reports, and I was sure he would be impressed by my experience.

"What mistakes?" Frank asked sounding irritated.

"Well, the gross margin table in this report doesn't calculate, for one thing," I said. "I think there's a typo in one of the numbers."

Frank pursed his lips and tilted his head sideways as he looked down at where I was pointing on the report. I was a little surprised at his reaction and even more so when he grabbed the papers abruptly and stared at the numbers I had circled in red.

"Please step into my office, Tanzie," he said.

I followed him in and he shut the door behind me.

I sat down, but Frank did not. His office was as utterly dull as its occupant. No framed jerseys on the wall or encased balls on this credenza. Just neat stacks of papers anchored with paperweights that I thought had been rendered obsolete with the onset of the technology age. There was a bookshelf, but so far Frank had not accumulated many materials worthy of display. Other than a framed photo of his bride on their wedding day, there were absolutely no personal items that might give insight into Frank's interests or hobbies. From what I now know about Frank, it is entirely possible that he has none.

"First of all," Frank said, "when you find something like that, you should never assume you're right. You should have said, 'Excuse me, Frank, but I am very confused about something in the report. I am not sure I understand how the gross margin table works.' Rather than accusing me of making an error. I didn't appreciate your tone."

This really caught me off guard. There is nothing remotely confusing about a typo. This was male dominating bullshit as far as I was concerned, and all the more galling being delivered by a thirty-something kid.

"I'm so sorry, Frank," I said. "I don't think making a typo is any big deal. I didn't mean to offend you." *Oh brother.* Right then I knew it was going to be torture tiptoeing around Frank and his inability to be wrong. It turned out all the reports had already been issued, and Frank had just been giving me busy work. He was horrified, too, that I corrected his grammar. Midwesterners in particular have a problem when it comes to the past participle of the verb "to go." They say, "I should have went there" or in Frank's case in this report, "The auditor had went to the job site to observe the inventory." I changed the "went" to "gone."

"You know, Tanzie," Frank pointed to my grammatical editing, "it's perfectly acceptable to use 'went' in that sentence. People say it all the time here. They know what I mean. Don't be acting like you're a smarty-pants or something."

At the time, I felt as though I had time traveled back to a middle school hallway. "Frank," I said, getting up to leave, "I am very confused about the spelling of Mr. Bishop's first name. I always thought there were two n's in Bennet, but of course he might have made a change. I can't be sure. I will be happy to follow up on that for you." I smiled pleasantly as I waited for a response from Frank, who was frantically looking at the reports to find that particular misspelling. "That will be all," he said finally, and I went back to my cube.

Moe is not much better than Frank. He's an entirely different kind of mediocrity. While Frank is the suit-and-tie type found throughout the world of finance, Moe is the blue-collar sort who brags about climbing up a twenty-five-foot tank or shooting the shit with the plant guys. He'll bend your ear during hunting season and keeps a shotgun in the back window of his mammoth, orange Ford 250 on oversized wheels with "MoPWR" license plates. Moe graduated from Oklahoma State and takes every opportunity to schmooze with Hal about the rivalry between the Pokes and the Sooners.

Moe is older and thicker than Frank, sporting one of those potbellies that hangs over his belt so he doesn't need to adjust his pants size as his girth expands over the years. My interview with Moe was memorable because he never asked me any questions.

"I've read your resume. Impressive. Now let me tell you about me," he began.

I smiled, relieved that I was off the hook about explaining why I was reentering the workforce but surprised nonetheless.

"I've been in this business for thirty years, and if you ask me, it's full of crooks. Top to bottom." He swiveled his chair toward his credenza and picked up one of the framed photos. "See this?" Moe handed me the picture. "That's me at my old job shaking hands with the CEO. The CEO of Midwestern Oilfield! I busted up a kickback ring in South Texas back in '07. Three hundred grand! Assholes are still in jail, thanks to yours truly."

I'd never heard the word "asshole" in a job interview before, but I stayed composed and gave a nod of interest.

"Wow!" I said, studying the photo long enough to feign admiration.

Moe took a used Kleenex out of his pants pocket and let out a productive blow, giving a final wipe on his sleeve before tossing the tissue in his wastebasket. He extended his hand to take back the picture and I bit my lower lip. I had encountered vagrants with better manners.

Moe then pointed to the wall behind me on which hung a framed cross-stitching that proclaimed, "Never try to teach a pig to sing. It wastes your time and it annoys the pig."

"See that?"

"It's lovely," I lied.

"My wife made that for me for Christmas one year. Words to live by."

"I'm not sure I understand." I really didn't. Clearly Moe was a pig. Still, I thought it interesting that his wife commemorated this shortcoming—and for Christmas, no less.

"Mark Twain said that. It means that you can't expect people to be something other than what they are. Don't expect everyone to be able to do everything. We need to coach the pig to be the very best pig and not waste our time on other things."

Sort of like making a mechanical engineer an expert on gas contracts, I guess. Moe spent the rest of the allotted interview time giving me the rundown on his days in the navy, his audit philosophy to find at least three "findings" before finishing any audit, and his preference for formalized communications. "I like everything in writing. CYA. Written proof."

"I'll remember that," I said, forcing a smile as he shook my hand when the Human Resources escort appeared at his office door.

Now, I look around the table as Moe gives his update and Hal nods while taking notes in a leather-bound diary.

"One more thing," Hal begins, and looks up from his notes. "We've been asked to look into gas contract settlements. It's pretty complicated stuff; I can tell you that from personal experience. I know you two are tied up." Hal looks at Moe and Frank, and I perk up. "I'm thinking of bringing in Boyd and Associates, your old firm, Frank." I look down at my notepad, trying not to telegraph my disappointment.

A few months back I approached Hal about wanting to take on some additional responsibility. I didn't mind doing the grunt work that I'd been doing, but my financial energy background made me a good fit to audit Bishop's energy trading organization or some higher risk areas than I was currently tackling. Hal politely asked me to sit, and in a loving, paternal way he told me a story.

"Tanzie," he said. "When my son Danny was sixteen and he got his driver's license, he begged me to let him drive my Corvette. I keep it just for weekends, you know. He begged me, Tanzie. He promised to be careful, not to speed, to take no other passengers along. I told him: 'Son, you do not have the *experience* to be trusted with something like that yet. You will someday; but not just yet.' You see, Tanzie, if I had given in, he would probably have done all those things. Not because he is a bad boy. No sir. Because he doesn't have enough *experience*. Being a good father means not giving everything all at once. That, girlie, is how to raise successful children and that is how you train people at work."

Did this man actually think of himself as my father? I was fifty-two years old, for heaven's sake. We were roughly the same age. I was at a loss for words. Actually, I had plenty of *experience*, certainly more than Frank or Moe. There was no point in arguing this, though. It would only have annoyed old Hal.

"Hal, thank you for your time. I hope someday you will see that I have developed enough experience to be trusted with a high performance audit and not wrap it around a tree." I smiled as I let myself out of his office.

◆

Our meeting is winding down and I shift in my chair in anticipation of my big moment. I feel sure that the results of my security audit will indicate to Hal that I have the *experience* and have "proven myself." Enough, anyway, to move up in the department or be given more complicated assignments—like gas contract settlements, perhaps.

"All right. Anything else?" Hal asks, signaling the end of the meeting.

"I want to give a brief update on the building security review I conducted over the weekend," I say.

"Please proceed," Hal says, looking at his watch.

"As you know, Moe asked me to perform an on-site review of building security." I look around the table: Frank is typing e-mails on his iPhone, and Moe has removed a Kleenex-wrapped pen from his ear and is examining the wax from multiple angles. I carry on with the report as rehearsed, trying not to become distracted by Moe's grooming ritual.

"I was able to penetrate the first level of security by informing the person on the security intercom that I was an employee and had forgotten my key card. I was clicked into the building without identifying myself. Once I was inside the building, a security guard was sent to escort me past security level two, the retractable flap barrier gate separating the lobby from the elevator bank. Once again, I was not asked for identification or credentials." I notice Hal looking at his watch again.

"Tanzie, could I ask you just to write a memo on this so we can discuss it at the closing meeting with the building security team?"

I see Frank and Hal suppress smirks as they glance at one another.

"Of course, Hal, but there were some rather disturbing findings yesterday."

"Such as?"

"The security guard asked me if I needed to go to the executive floors."

Frank looks up from his phone, and Moe puts his pen down.

"What did you say?" Hal asks.

"I said yes. He never asked for a driver's license or even a business card. He took me all the way to thirty and never once asked who I was."

"Thirty! You went to thirty?"

"I didn't think I would get there when I said it. I assumed he would require some ID or call the Building Services Director, like the protocol requires, but he didn't. We just got in the elevator and rode up there, and—"

"You didn't get out, did you?" Moe interrupts.

"Yes, I did, and he just left me there."

"Alone?"

"Yes, alone. He just got back in the elevator and left me there all by myself."

"Are you sure?" Frank asks.

"As confusing as all this was, yes, Frank, I am sure that yesterday I was left unattended on the executive floor with full access to every office." I catch myself; the sarcastic tone might undermine my success here.

"You didn't go into any offices did you?" asks a nervous Moe as he rolls a tiny wax ball between his fingers.

I take a breath. Things are not going quite as planned.

"No. But I could tell they were open, though, just by looking down the hallway."

"Then you just left . . . right?" Hal leans slightly toward me.

"Um, right," I lie. "I just called the elevator, rode down, and had the guard let me out." I can tell that I am in trouble. All my preparation had assumed that my information would be favorably received.

"For pity's sake, Tanzie. What were you thinking? What if you had run into one of the executives? What would you have said? That I sent one of my auditors up there to snoop around? How would that make me look?" Hal's bald head turns red, and Moe shifts in his chair, visibly uncomfortable at having his underling blindside him at a meeting by having—in his view, anyway—so clearly misunderstood his direction.

"Hal, I thought it would be in management's best interest to understand any existing vulnerabilities so they could remedy them before someone with sinister motives could exploit them."

"Why didn't you call me before you got on the elevator, Tanzie?" Moe chimes in.

"You really shouldn't have went up there without checking first," Frank agrees.

"So the guard asks if I want to go up to the executive floor, and I say, 'Just a minute, let me call and ask someone'?"

"No, Tanzie." Moe leans toward me pointing his finger. "You should have stopped right there. Once he asked you, that was enough for the report. Why can't you see that?"

I think, *Because, Moe, then we wouldn't know that the guard would leave me alone on thirty, or that Marla leaves her password unsecured.* But I can't explain that to him now. If just being in the foyer on thirty causes this kind of ruckus, then snooping around, no matter how productive it had been, would send these guys through the roof and me out to the unemployment line.

"Don't be so hard on Tanzie, fellas," Hal says, settling into his fatherly tone. "What this is telling us is that Tanzie doesn't have good judgment just yet. We need to be mindful when giving her assignments that may be above her skill level. Now Tanzie," Hal says, looking me in the eye, "I want you to write up your notes on this, but just stop when the guard *asks* you if you would like to go up to the executive floors. Are we clear about that?"

I cannot help the stunned look that is surely plain on my face by now. I am totally lost in anger, and I know I need to disengage.

"Of course," I begin. "Would you mind if I excuse myself to get started on that?"

"Good idea, Tanzie," Hal nods. "I'm sure we've all learned a valuable lesson here. Am I right, boys?"

Frank and Moe nod, and I get up, smooth my skirt, and walk out of Hal's office and back to my cube.

What just went on in there? I ask myself, rubbing my head with my hands, realizing afterward that I have probably smeared mascara all over my face. Under normal circumstances I would dash off to the ladies' room to clean up, but I cannot muster the energy.

———◆———

When Hal's office door opens a few minutes later, Moe stops by my cube and continues the reprimand. "I'll take it from here," he tells me at the end of it, and with that I am dumped from helping him with his audit and reassigned to work for Frank. I feel my face get red and hold back tears at the idea of having failed so publicly.

How can I resurrect my career working for bumpkins incapable of thinking beyond a checklist? I think I have uncovered a major security lapse, and instead of accolades, I am bawled out and taken off the assignment. From experience, I know that it's best to just move on and wait for another opportunity to shine and redeem myself—I'll keep my head down and keep doing my job—but for right now, I am devastated.

Working in a cube provides no privacy, so I walk quickly down the hall for a five-minute cool down in the ladies' room. When I return, my raccoon eyes are replaced by red puffy ones, and Frank shows up at my desk with a stack of files for me to scan.

"This shouldn't take long," I say. "Do you have anything else for me to work on?"

"Not sure. I might have some more filing or document scanning I can send your way. Just sit tight for now."

Sit tight means sitting there and doing nothing until he is ready to show me what he wants me to do for him. I sit tight until 11:30, at which time I knock on Frank's office door and ask if it is okay for me to go to lunch. It's a courtesy most young people don't observe nowadays. That is one of my redeeming qualities: old-fashioned business manners. I always make sure to ask Frank or Moe, depending on which I am working for, because it makes them feel important and reinforces their superiority. And sure enough, Frank beams as he tells me it is okay for me to go to lunch.

I usually eat at my desk, but today I need to get away. I am too mad to be hungry, but I power-eat two burritos from the food truck outside our building as I walk six blocks to a pocket park with a bench. I break tradition by smoking three cigarettes in a row, hoping that the stiff Oklahoma breeze will carry the residual stink elsewhere. As I walk back to the office, I munch on a couple of Altoids for dessert and am back in my cube ready to continue to sit tightly until summoned.

After a half hour, I overhear Frank tell Hal that he is off to a meeting with the financial group for the rest of the afternoon, which makes it clear that I will not be getting any more assignments that day. It is not unusual for Moe or Frank just to leave me idle for extended periods. As the underling in the department, they view me as dispensable.

I decide to spend my remaining time looking at my Windows XP bible. It is a thick yellow instruction book that explains how to use a desktop computer in the simplest terms for the non-techie. Most companies have moved to at least Windows 7, but not Bishop, where technology is viewed as something for lightweights. "If 20 columnar pads were good enough for us in the '70s . . ." I heard the CFO say at an employee meeting once. But although it is archaic, the operating system is still more advanced than what I am used to. I goof around, changing the displays: large font, tiny font, blue background, purple wavy background. I find the date and time function and change that too. I set the date to June 1, 2007, and the time to 6:00 p.m.: my fiftieth birthday party.

Winston had surprised me by gathering our friends at the club for a party. It was a sweet gesture on his part, particularly since we had grown so far apart over the years. My friends Beth McAfee and Alice Mayhew had been enlisted to help with the details and to refine a guest list that included fifteen other couples, mostly from the club. The cocktail hour was out on a covered patio overlooking the eighteenth green, and conversation circles formed as hors d'oeuvres were passed among the guests.

"Happy birthday, Tanzie!" Alice squealed and gave me a kiss on the cheek. Her face had some sunburn peeking through her makeup and her bare shoulders had a white outline of a sleeveless golf shirt.

"Did you two play today?" I asked Alice and Ken.

"Oh my God, Tanzie. I knew I shouldn't have worn

this dress with my golfer tan." Alice shrugged and laughed. "Oh well."

"How'd you play?" I continued.

"Uhhhh. Forty on the front. Fifty-nine on the back! Totally cratered." Alice giggled. She wasn't much of a golfer, but Winston and I played with the Mayhews every Sunday in the couples' tournament.

"Good grief, Alice. How do you shoot a forty, fifty-nine?" I shook my head laughing.

"Got on every green in regulation on the front, hit in every lake and sand trap on the back. That's how. I think I just got tired."

"I think you're a sandbagger, Alice." Winston laughed. "Driving up your handicap so we can win on Sundays." He leaned toward Alice. "Atta girl."

"Ken shot a seventy-one!" Alice smiled at her husband.

"Good man." Winston gave Ken a slap on the back. "We'll see if you can keep that up tomorrow morning."

"Better bring your wallet, Winston. I mean to win back the five grand you won last week!" Ken joked.

Alice was like another sister to me, and I spent countless afternoons hanging out at their sprawling home in Memorial playing with the boys when they were toddlers and helping them with their math homework when they grew older. Winston and I were godparents to Matt, the older boy. "Your godson; my goddamn son," Alice would joke when Matt was going through an episode of teenage obnoxiousness.

Ken and Winston had been high school buddies

at St. John's, an exclusive Houston prep school, and they remained best friends throughout their professional lives.

Grant and Beth McAfee and Bill and Julie Matheson strolled over to join the conversation. Handshakes, kisses, and birthday wishes gave way to cocktail banter about the condition of the greens, a new club chef, and a proposed capital assessment to widen cart paths.

Ken, Winston, Grant, and Bill called themselves the "Rat Pack" and had a standing tee time on Saturday mornings. They played for high stakes and were considered the power foursome at Ravenswood, our club. Each had served a term as president and their portraits hung in the main hallway. As the men discussed club business, we women snuck away for our own conversation.

"Tanzie, I signed us up for the shootout tournament in two weeks. That's still good for you, right?" Beth asked as she lit up a cigarette, waving the smoke away as she exhaled. The shootout was an annual club tournament benefiting one of Beth's many charities. We were always tournament partners because we had single-digit handicaps, thrived on pressure and competition, and dominated most of the tournament play at Ravenswood.

"Absolutely! Who are you playing with, Alice?" I asked. Though she and I were best friends, she wasn't serious about her golf and tended to lose focus and to clown around, which explained her horrendous back nine. She didn't seem to mind that I paired up with Beth in tournaments; in fact, Alice probably preferred it, since she really hated playing under pressure.

"I'm playing with Frankie Waldon. We'll have a good time in the fourth flight, us high handicappers."

"Frankie cheats," Beth whispered.

"Good," said Alice. "I could use the help."

"Alice!" Beth and I shouted in unison. Golfing is a game of honor and cheating is unthinkable. It's a swift road to being ostracized at a club. Sandbagging is one thing, but no serious golfer will tolerate cheating.

"I'll keep an eye on her. Don't worry." Alice rolled her eyes. "She's still a blast to play with. More fun than you two, that's for sure."

"How about you, Julie?" Alice asked. Beth and I didn't care too much for Julie Matheson, but because our husbands were close friends, she came along with the package. Julie was always complaining about aches and pains and had a tendency to back out of social engagements at the last minute. Alice was too nice of a person to get annoyed by such minor things.

"Bad back." Julie sighed. "I'll try to help with the sign-in, but I can't promise anything."

There were other guests to mingle with, so I excused myself and rejoined Winston, who was talking with Mason, one of our older friends who had suffered a series of strokes lately and was prone to inappropriate remarks. "So how's the new CFO—Caroline, is it?— working out, Winston? She's pretty damn young, don't you think?" asked Mason. "She's a rock star," said Winston. "Battle-tested over at KPMG, made partner over there in eight years. I think that may be a firm record."

"Unbelievable. Maybe she has her sights on your job. How long do you think before she's the next CEO?" Mason joked, as his wife, Leanne, looked on uncomfortably.

"No doubt, Mason, I'll need to watch my step around the board," said Winston, always the politician.

"Not bad looking, either," said Mason. "Must be more enjoyable jetting off to New York with her instead of that old fart, George Callaway."

Winston looked a bit startled but composed himself. "I can assure you, it's all business, Mason. George was a great executive to work with."

Leanne gave Mason a gentle nudge and changed the subject. "Tanzie, I'm wondering if I can borrow you to look over the luncheon menu for the bridge group next week. It'll only take a second."

While there had been many previous infidelities on Winston's part, I was blissfully unaware of this affair that would change my life so profoundly a year later. I didn't get the inference underlying Mason's comments until many months afterward. Looking back, I think plenty of people did know, but that is how country club friendships work, sometimes. They tend to be superficial and husband-centered. The women are your friends while you're married and involved in the club, but since the man is the member and the woman a "spouse," a divorce means that you are no longer welcome on the premises. No Wednesday morning golf, no ladies association lunches, no bridge or book club. Promises to meet outside the club evaporate over time, and pretty soon you lose all contact.

Still, my friendship with Beth and Alice was anything but superficial, and we remained close even through the awkward months as the divorce finalized. I promised to keep in touch after moving to Tulsa but instead retreated inward. I can't pinpoint the emotion that made me distance myself from my closest friends. Alice suggested I join Facebook, but I didn't. She and Beth left messages on my machine and sent e-mail that I didn't return. I fell into a funk after moving, and reminders of my old life only made me more depressed.

And the whole process had started right then—June 1, 2007, my fiftieth birthday. I stare at the date, right there on my computer clock.

Moe and Hal stop by on their way out the door, interrupting my thoughts. "Just so you know," Moe begins, "I called around about the security breach over the weekend. The guy they used was new because of the holiday. They don't think that will happen again."

"Okay," I reply. "I am really sorry if I went too far. Are you sure there isn't anything I can help you with on your audit, Moe?"

"Maybe. I'll let you know," he says coldly.

Hal leans in. "Tanzie, could you put together a data request for this construction audit before you go home tonight? See if we can get the contracts by the end of the week. Think you can do that?"

"Of course, I'll send the requests by e-mail tonight. I'll copy you so you can make sure I did it correctly," I say, trying not to sound angry.

I get busy putting together a schedule and figuring out who has the needed information as the clock reaches five and keeps going. *Ironic*, I think, *I had nothing to do all day but will end up leaving late because of this assignment. I feel sure this isn't accidental.* I click *send* and pack up for the day.

CHAPTER FOUR

After I finish my dinner, I pour another glass of wine and head out to my balcony for my evening smoke, taking the landline with me. It has been an exhausting day and I want to talk to someone. I think about calling Alice or Beth, but that feels funny after blowing them off for the last six months. Instead, I decide to talk to my sister again.

Lucy and I are Irish twins, just eleven months apart. Looking at us, though, it's hard to believe we're related, let alone sisters. Lucy is tall and delicate with red hair, and I am sturdy, dark, and athletic—good peasant stock, my brother Charlie used to tease. Lucy and I are the youngest in our family of seven girls and one boy, with an immigrant Irish dad and Greek mother. We grew up in the Richmond District in San Francisco, the set of avenues just north of Golden Gate Park and east of the Pacific. The O'Learys were not dirt poor but more on the "barely scraping by" rung of the economic ladder. Often the recipients of charity donations, we volunteered our time at church projects to compensate for our inability to make monetary contributions; our ultimate donation was my oldest sister, Honey, to the convent, which allowed the rest of us to receive a subsidized education at Catholic schools.

Growing up, I never knew what loneliness was. But tonight, on my balcony looking at Utica Square below full of people shopping and meeting friends for drinks or dinner, I feel completely isolated and long to be back home. I close my eyes for a moment trying to remember the smells and sounds of my childhood.

"Tanzie. Tanzie. Are you awake?" Lucy raised my eyelid with her finger.

I swatted her hand away and opened my eyes on my own, groaning as I stared up at the nearly twenty years' worth of petrified chewing gum stuck to the underside of our dining room table, placed there pre-dinner by my siblings. I had seen it before. As the two youngest, Lucy and I were the most portable, so even though we fell asleep in our own bed, there was no guarantee we would awaken there the next morning. Our bed was routinely reassigned to accommodate the many visitors to the O'Leary home.

As immigrants, my parents felt a responsibility to help not just their own family members coming to America but also people in general coming to San Francisco. At any given time, entire families of cousins, friends of cousins, and other nonrelatives crammed into our home. When couch space filled up, the children were redistributed to unconventional sleeping spaces.

Lucy and I crawled out from our makeshift bed in hand-me-down flannel nightgowns and headed through the kitchen and onto the enclosed back porch that functioned as our laundry room.

"Here's your uniform." Lucy handed me a wrinkled blue plaid jumper from the pile of clothes that had been dumped out of the dryer onto the floor, and I got busy hunting for a blouse, underwear, and socks. Our mother always made sure our clothes were clean, but the final steps of the laundry process were rarely completed in time to be of any use.

"Want me to iron your stuff?" I asked Lucy.

"It's okay. I don't mind the wrinkles," she replied, stripping down and throwing on her clothes in almost a single motion.

"Lucy! You can't go to school like that. Your socks don't even match." She gave a shrug and left me on the porch standing on a box at the ironing board. Even at six years old, I understood the value of good presentation. So, even though my jumper was two versions behind the current uniform worn at St. Geronimo's Catholic School and had been worn by six previous sisters, it would be starched and crisp when I arrived on the playground that morning.

In the time it took me to get dressed on the porch, the downstairs had transformed from total quiet to complete chaos. Every chair at the Formica dining room table was now occupied. Uncle Agamemnon was arguing with a distant cousin from County Cork about whether Richard Nixon was finished politically, and my brother and two of our older sisters were retelling jokes from last night's *Ed Sullivan Show*. My mother had two coffee pots percolating on the kitchen stove, and a line of visitors waited with coffee mugs in hand. Some strange old man in a black suit was smoking and sitting off by himself on a kitchen stool, holding the yellow clay ashtray I'd made in art class on his lap. I found Lucy sitting Indian style under the table with a bowl of cereal between her legs and a book in her hand. I joined her.

"Greek myths," she answered without me asking.

"Read it to me," I pleaded.

As a second grader, Lucy was reading at a high school level and always seemed to have her nose in a book. I, too, was an avid reader, but since there was only one book and two of us, it would be better for her to narrate rather than have me read over her shoulder. The story was about Hermes and the Cattle of Apollo, and I ate her cereal as she read.

"Time for school," Mama shouted. "The bell rings in ten minutes!"

Lucy and I emerged from under the table leaving the book and bowl, which I was certain would still be there when we returned home.

Lucy answers on the second ring and I begin to cry as I recount my horrible day.

"Just quit, Tanzie. Come out here and live with me."

"Thanks, but living in a trailer might be the final straw."

"What was I thinking? There probably isn't enough room for all your shoes and purses, anyway."

"Hey, Lucy, I just want my career back."

"I know what you mean."

I was taken aback by the remark. With all my focus on my own career woes, I'd completely forgotten about my sister's failed business. Back in the '90s Lucy gained considerable fame and fortune by inventing cotton that grew naturally in colors. Inventing seems like the wrong word, because she actually patented her seeds after painstakingly crossbreeding season after season, extracting the genetic properties of most value to her. She had started with some brown wild cotton that was thought to be pest resistant but too short-stapled to be spun commercially.

As she selectively bred for length she discovered quite unexpectedly that the brown hue contained a spectrum of other colors that could be extracted through selective breeding techniques. This is not genetic engineering, mind you, which shortcuts the process and can result in dangerous and unanticipated results. Lucy's technique, while arguably slow, partnered with nature so that all her results were in keeping with her environmental and scientific ethics. It was along the lines of utilizing a wise and experienced matchmaker versus cloning human beings.

Her business prospered for a while until she received some bad advice from Winston, of all people. Though Lucy had not liked what my ex-husband stood for environmentally, she had respected his Rice MBA and business acumen. Prior to his interference, Lucy had planned a season in advance, gotten contracts with her buyers, and grown to order. No risk. Winston advised her to speculate by planting crops and building an inventory so that the accelerated turnaround could be used to bring in buyers who did not want to wait a season or be exposed to crop failures or other delays. The advice made sense on paper but was a disaster once implemented. Poor Lucy got caught in a global cotton glut and had not been able to cover the cost of growing or storing her product.

In exactly two years from the day she began to implement Winston's strategy, her business had gone bankrupt, and she bought a little farm in Northern California with what little she had left. Now, she grows a little cotton on the side to sell to craftsmen and hand spinners, but any dreams she had of being a global presence in the world of agriculture and textiles are gone. Retired to her farm and without capital or the energy to restart her business, Lucy has poured herself into environmental causes, raising sheep and chickens, and volunteering at her organic co-op. To her credit, Lucy has never taken her aggravation out on me, although I could not help but feel somewhat responsible.

"Looks like Winston screwed us both out of careers," Lucy concludes, and I start to laugh. I can hear her chuckling on the other end.

"Why don't you come to Tulsa, Lucy? Come visit me," I plead.

"I really can't leave the farm. It's so hard to find anyone to take over. Besides, you'll be just fine, Tanzie. Don't you remember your babysitting empire? You're so driven. Just give it some time."

"Oh God, Lucy. Yes, climbing a corporate ladder is exactly like cultivating babysitting clients." The sarcasm makes Lucy pause at the other end and I can tell I've hurt her feelings a little.

"You know what I mean, Tanzie," Lucy resumes. As the youngest of the seven girls, I inherited a babysitting dynasty whose client list had been refined over the years to include the who's who of San Francisco. For fifty cents an hour, an O'Leary girl would watch the children, feed, bathe, and put them to bed, plus clean the house. Lucy hated taking care of children. Money was not a motivator for her, but it had been for me, so I happily absorbed her client base, working just about every night, spending my evenings in the orderly and quiet homes of my wealthy clients. After I put the children to bed and cleaned up, I could have privacy, something that was impossible at my house. As a teenager, when I had envisioned my future, it was not sitting at a Formica table drinking coffee and listening to a distant relative snore on the couch.

"Maybe I should go back to babysitting. It's not too far from what I'm doing at Bishop. And it pays about the same."

"What do you do, exactly? Break into buildings?" Lucy is not a corporate person and her only exposure to auditors is via the IRS.

"Well, in most public companies, Internal Audit is an independent group that reports directly to the board of directors. It's charged with identifying unknown risks, processes that need improvement, and disconnects between what the board thinks is happening and what really is happening."

"Like the company fuzz? You must be popular." Lucy laughs.

"Yes, it is quite the social repellant. But it's project based and we get to do a lot of different things. I think it's interesting."

"Right." Her sarcastic tone comes through loud and clear.

I continue to describe my job in greater detail than Lucy wants to hear. I tell her that since Bishop is not a public company, the department is less independent than what I have been describing.

"Hal reports to the Chief Compliance Officer, an attorney pretty far down in the organization. We look mainly at policy compliance: Have people fudged their expense reports or used their company credit cards for personal benefit? We also look at field operations for safety violations as well as construction contracts to make sure our contractors are billing us properly and have adequate insurance. We're not necessarily encouraged to look very hard."

The consensus is that Bishop has miserable controls. The brothers pride themselves on being low-cost providers to the industry, and that means no unnecessary administrative personnel. Accounting departments are thinly staffed and capable of performing only the most critical functions. Engineering staff, responsible for reviewing bills charged to capital construction projects, work late nights just making sure the pipelines are being laid or the plants are getting built on schedule. Cost analysis takes a backseat and is cursory at best. Bishop is making plenty of money, so there's no perceived need to burn up resources chasing problems that don't exist.

"Hey, do you remember what tomorrow is?" I guess Lucy must have had enough of my lecture.

"April 6th? Oh, Mama's birthday."

"She'd have been ninety-two. I've been so sad today. I still miss her."

"Oh Lucy, all I've done is talk about me this whole time." I'd forgotten all about our mother. Once again I am reminded of my selfishness. Not that I was unloved, but Lucy was our mother's clear favorite. Lucy is beautiful and kind while I am aggressive, cunning, and selfish. "You're going to have a hard time finding a man to put up with you, Tanzie!" my mother would often chide.

I remember when I was in the fifth grade St. Geronimo's had a contest to see which student could sell the most raffle tickets for the spring carnival. The winner would get first pick at a prize table full of things our family could never afford. The clear choice, in my view, was a beanbag chair in red vinyl. Seating space was at a premium in our house, and having your own personal chair would be huge. Plus it was portable, so I would be guaranteed a seat in any room. Lucy and I got busy selling tickets, as did a few of my other sisters still at St. Geronimo's. The competition was fierce and there were many fights and tears leading up to the contest deadline. Lucy and I were neck and neck and each kept our final tallies secret from the other. We were standing outside at assembly when Sister Mary Eucharist read the results.

"First place goes to Lucy O'Leary, grade six."

I was shocked. Then mad. Lucy was going to get my chair. The jealousy made me cry as I watched my older sister survey the prize table. To my amazement, she selected a huge bottle of perfume. The girl who came to school in a wrinkled uniform picks the perfume? It made no sense.

"Second place goes to Tanzie O'Leary, grade five."
I wiped my eyes and made a beeline for the chair. I got what I wanted and was elated.

"Why did you pick the perfume, Lucy?" I asked when we began to walk home that afternoon.

"Mama's birthday is tomorrow. She told me once that she loved perfume, but I know we never have enough money to splurge on it."

CHAPTER FIVE

A lovely part of the aging process—besides weight gain, stiffness, and memory lapses—is its effect on your sleep habits. Sometimes I awake in a pool of sweat and feel as though it is a perpetual Houston August in my bed. This morning, I step out to my balcony to cool off and then go to my tiny kitchen for some ice water. It is just past 4:00 a.m., and I am flipping through the channels on the flat screen, waiting for my temperature to reboot, when my interest is snagged by CNN showing a massive fire in a residential area of Houston. I cover my mouth in horror and turn up the sound.

I walk closer to the screen to see if I can pick out any landmarks. It is still dark outside except for the enormous flames, but I can see the seventy-story Williams Tower and the Southwest Freeway/Loop 610 intersection. The fire looks like it is within a half mile of the Galleria shopping mall. *Oh my God!* I think, *I know people who live near there!*

On TV, the anchor is interviewing a resident of the area.

"I heard an explosion," the man says. "It shook my whole house and I could smell smoke. I grabbed my dog and ran outside. My roof was on fire, but the big stuff was down the block from me, where those fancy new townhouses and condos are. I tell you what—I have never seen anything like that before in my life, and I'm a Vietnam vet. There were injured people running down the street with third-degree burns."

The CNN news team spends the next thirty minutes or so speculating about causes—pipeline explosion or terrorism or possibly a plane crash—and casualty figures—massive, given the high-density housing that has sprung up in that area recently and the fact that the tragedy occurred in the middle of the night when families were home in bed. Hospitals are reporting in about the terrible injuries and are asking for blood donations.

I think about friends of mine—Beth and Grant and Ken and Alice—and wonder whether they are okay. I think about where they live in Houston, relative to the fire. Even given the scale of this thing, it doesn't seem as if any of them are in any immediate danger. I force myself not to worry about it right now. Surely they are safe. Still, there is no going back to bed, and I'm an early riser anyway, so I make a pot of coffee and wait for the sun to come up. I sit glued to the television but get frustrated because there's no real information, just speculative chatter between newscasters. I decide to take a shower and get ready for work, but with the sour feeling in my stomach, I elect not to eat breakfast or indulge in my morning cigarette. *Those poor people in Houston. Maybe I could give blood up here in Tulsa, if only as a gesture.*

The ten-story Bishop garage is located directly across the street from the main building. An underground tunnel connects it to the main building in case of bad weather. Generally, though, I prefer to take the aboveground route. I pull into the garage around 6:30 and drive up the inclines to the fifth floor so that I can park right by the elevator. Even though there are plenty of spots on the lower floors, I find that unless I park in the same spot every day, I have serious trouble remembering where I left my car. Aging is so much fun. By going to the fifth floor, I am guaranteed the same spot, even when I'm running late.

As I get out of my car, a sporty red Mercedes convertible drives by—*unusual that an executive would get here this early and park this high in the garage*, I think. But when the car stops, the woman getting out does not fit an executive profile. She is about my age, and she wears an outfit that combines pants with a sort of coordinated top—Garanimals for adults, as I heard someone call the style once. Her hair looks home-dyed with that out-of-the-box color and is not professionally styled. I push the ground button on the elevator and extend my hand to the woman.

"Hi, I am Tanzie Lewis; I don't think we've met. I'm fairly new here."

"Mazie Caldwell, Accounts Payable. I've been here going on five years."

"Oh my. Nice car you got there. Do you park up here so it won't get dinged by all those huge pickup trucks?"

She looks a little uncomfortable for a moment and then recovers. "That was my midlife crisis present to myself," she explains.

"I was left some money when my uncle in New Orleans died, God rest his soul."

"Pretty nice. That'll take the edge off a hot flash."

"Ha, yes it does. Thank you very much. You have a nice car, too, Tanzie. Is that your Lexus?"

"Rich ex-husband who, sadly, is still alive."

The garage elevator doors open and I can see news crews crowding the front of our building getting ready for a morning broadcast. Each of the three major networks, along with affiliates for CNN and FOX, appears to have a reporter standing by.

"What's that all about?" I ask Mazie.

"I surely don't know."

We cross the street, and I stop a cameraman on his way to a van.

"What's going on?" I ask as he opens the back gate and pulls out an extension cord and a plastic utility box of some sort.

"Bishop pipeline exploded in Houston this morning."

"That was ours?!" I look at Mazie but she doesn't seem to have a clue. "Are you sure?" I ask, almost shouting at the cameraman, but he just ignores me and walks over to his reporter, who is adjusting her earpiece.

We enter the Bishop lobby, flashing our key cards past the security gate leading to the elevators. I fill Mazie in on what I had learned that morning while we walk over to the elevator bank.

"This can't be good for us. Hope we don't lose our jobs," she says.

"I hadn't thought of that. But I guess you're right."

"We'll just have to say a prayer to Jesus that the Bishops can help us through this and that we all come out okay."

You might want to include something about the folks in Houston who have more to worry about than a job, I think to myself, hoping Mazie cannot detect my amazement at her Christian selfishness from the look on my face.

"By the way, Tanzie," she continues, "since you're new here and all, I would like to invite you to join me for services at the Broken Arrow Church of Redemption some Sunday. We have this new young pastor from Dallas, and he is simply wonderful, and our congregation is great. The Easter service this year was unbelievable. Would you like to join me next Sunday?"

"That is so nice, but I am attending services with my new neighbor at the South Tulsa Pentecostal church. I will let you know if I feel like venturing out."

"Well, we're having our Spring Fun Day a week from next Saturday, and I'm the fundraising chair. You need to come by. Donna Douglas—she played Elly May Clampett on *The Beverly Hillbillies*—she'll be there to sign autographs."

"Wish I could, but I have plans. Maybe next time."

"Okay, then, it was nice to meet you. Have a blessed day," she says as I exit the elevator on six.

"You too, Mazie," I reply, looking back with a forced smile.

Almost no one is in yet, which I don't mind. I like getting to the office before the others, anyway. The extra time allows me to linger over a cup of coffee, read the *Wall Street Journal*, and review my agenda for the day. Today, though, feels more urgent, and I dash to my desk to get on the Internet.

Google News doesn't have too much new information about the Houston explosion, other than a statement that it was in fact a gas pipeline operated by Bishop that caused the explosion. There is an e-mail from Bishop's corporate communications reminding us that company policy precludes employees from discussing company events with the media and that all questions should be directed to the public relations group. There is another company communication from Bennet Bishop reemphasizing the company's commitment to safety and his deep personal sorrow for what has happened in Houston.

But there is something funny about the e-mail. According to my inbox, it shows a received date of June 2, 2007, at 4:00 a.m. rather than today's date, April 6, 2010. After a moment and a couple more sips of coffee, I remember having fooled around with my date function in Windows. Could that affect the date of an e-mail? I check my send box and notice that the e-mail requesting Hal's data from yesterday also has the wrong date. I go into the settings mode and change the date and clock back to the correct time. The sent and received e-mails retain their incorrect dates. *How weird.*

I call Cindy, the file clerk I had e-mailed about the contracts. I know she generally gets in early, and when I ask her about the e-mail, she indicates that she has just seen it this morning and will get me the information as soon as she can.

"Great, but what is the date on the e-mail?" I ask.

"Yesterday," she says, annoyed that I am pestering her.

"Sorry," I say. "Just let me know when you have the files ready; I'll be happy to stop by and pick them up."

I have never read anywhere that the desktop clock of the person who sends an e-mail regulates the date on the correspondence itself. I spend the next hour changing the clock back and forth and sending myself e-mails from my company e-mail to my Gmail account, testing out how the process works. As an auditor, I always thought that the date on an e-mail was factual evidence documenting when a communication has occurred. I guess I never realized it could be manipulated so easily.

Most companies have adopted a policy of purging all e-mail every ninety days to save storage space on servers, so a retained e-mail from one side of the correspondence might be considered adequate evidence by some investigators.

Soon everyone has filed into work, and the office staff is buzzing about the explosion in Houston—how awful it is and what it will do to the company. Like Mazie, most of the employees are focused on their own lives rather than the out-of-towners. They are right to worry, though, since Bishop is a major employer in Tulsa, and something like this could certainly result in cutbacks and layoffs. While a pipeline explosion is always bad news, one with significant loss of human life trumps environmental destruction any day. Plus, these were not just any humans; they were rich Texans with enough resources to go after the damned Okies that had caused this disaster. It is too early to know what actually caused the explosion. It could have been any number of things: a construction crew negligently digging, terrorism, or a break due to corrosion. One thing is certain: Every lawyer from LA to New York will be trying to get a piece of the action, and every insurance company from London to Hartford will be trying to find a way to contain the losses.

I decide to call some of my Houston friends at lunch and get the lowdown from them. Personal calls are discouraged during work hours, and cube life makes such infractions noticeable and reportable by anyone hoping to out the auditor who's breaking company policy.

Frank arrives around eight thirty and calls me to his office.

"Did you hear about the explosion?" he asks as he hangs his jacket up and sits down at his desk.

"Yes, I have friends who live in that area, but so far I haven't heard anything. I may make some calls at lunch, if that's all right."

"Make sure you don't say anything inappropriate, Tanzie. The press is all over this."

"Yes, Frank." There is nothing quite as irritating as being spoken to like a child by a thirty-year-old twit. "I read the e-mail, but thank you for reminding me."

"I have a vendor setup test for you to do, since you were pulled from the office security review."

Thanks for reminding me.

"Take a look," he continues, "and let me know if you have any questions or need some help getting started."

I take the audit program and give it a quick read. Obviously I cannot be relied on to exercise prudent judgment, so Frank is making sure I know exactly what to do this time by writing it all out. Still, not wanting to repeat my previous *mistake*, I read it three times over before leaving Frank's office. I need to select twenty new vendor setups and make sure they have been properly approved. Easy enough.

In a large company, vendors are set up in the system so they can be automatically paid when an invoice comes in. One of the oldest fraud schemes around is to enter a fictitious vendor into the system and then send in phony invoices, which get paid automatically to the fraudster.

"Frank, I notice that you only want me to check that the vendor information was approved prior to setup. Did you want me to validate the vendors through Dun & Bradstreet? Also, should I look at changes to remittance addresses or wire instructions, or just new vendors? I did this sort of testing such a long time ago . . . and it is very confusing. I just want to make sure I don't leave something out."

Frank looks at me, irritated. "Let me noodle on that, Tanzie. Just do the testing as written for now, and I'll get back to you."

"Will do." I make a quick exit, rolling my eyes once my back is turned.

Back at my desk, I get busy organizing the list of data I will need to request for Frank's test. I pick up the phone and dial one of the very few work numbers that is worth memorizing.

"Help Desk. This is Todd."

"Hi Todd, it's Tanzie. Can you send me a data dump of all the new vendors set up in the Master File since the beginning of the year to today?"

"Sure thing. I'll put a ticket in for you. Now, I can't pull just new vendors, so the dump will include all changes to the Master File. To get just the new vendors, you'll have to do a pivot or write a macro to pull just the additions."

"No problem," I say, "I've been schooled by the master."

Todd laughs. "Right." Todd graduated in 2008 with an information systems degree and had been recruited for a job at the IT Help Desk. I have a standing date to treat Todd to coffee on Wednesdays in exchange for his tutoring me on my woefully ancient IT skills. Todd has demonstrated extraordinary patience in walking me through the complexities of writing Excel macros and creating pivot tables so that I can play catch-up with the rest of the team. After four months of working with Todd, I have surpassed the skill sets of Hal, Frank, and Moe combined and become the go-to gal when some complex schedule or document is necessary.

I occasionally bake cupcakes and other treats and leave them for Todd and the other young men in the technology group. They are especially grateful and as a result give preference to my requests over all others.

"When do you need this by?" he asks me now.

"How soon can I get it?"

"It shouldn't take long," he says. "I can have it ready for you in a few minutes or so. Tanzie, you're from Houston, right? I was thinking of you when I heard the news. Did you know any of the people hurt this morning?"

Finally, someone is looking beyond himself.

"I don't think so, Todd, but thanks for asking."

"Let me know if you need anything else."

I hang up the phone feeling the first bit of calmness since turning on the TV this morning.

Shortly, a ping on my email indicates that, as promised, my request has been granted quickly, and I download the Excel file to take a look. Todd is right—the file is huge. There are twenty-nine column headings that include all sorts of vendor information, names, reference numbers, and tax IDs, as well as banking and wire instructions. This many rows of changes—7,223 rows, to be exact—exceeds my ability to make any sense of the data or even make a selection for Frank's test, so I start to put a macro together that will identify only the new vendors. Still, I am surprised to see so many changes in a four-month window.

Bishop is huge, but this is more activity than seems possible. My curiosity piqued, I start filtering and making pivot tables to analyze the file. Most of the changes have been made to the remittance address, and I filter those to understand why the volume is so high. What's really strange is that many of these changes involve the same three vendors, and the addresses have been changed several times a week.

The vendors are AT&T, Grainger (a tool company used by the field locations), and Oklahoma Power, which is the utility provider not just for our office but also for all the plants and field offices in Oklahoma. The other strange thing about the activity is that the addresses have not been changed permanently; instead, the same two addresses have just been switched back and forth. Further, the changes have all been made under the same user ID: MCALDWELL. Mazie Caldwell—the lady with the really nice Mercedes whom I'd just met in the parking lot. *Classic*, I think. *Remittance information for vendors often changes, but not weekly and not back and forth. This is definitely a red flag noting suspicious activity.*

"Hi, Todd, it's me again. Can I get a data dump of all payments made to vendors set up by user name MCALDWELL since inception? That should be about five years. There are some cupcakes in it for you and the gang if you can get that out to me by lunch."

"In that case, you can have it there in about five minutes. Make them with that chocolate icing, please—mmmmmmmmm."

"Deal! Thanks again, Todd—you're the best!"

My review of the payment information confirms my suspicions. Starting about four years ago, judging by the data I'm looking at, Mazie has stolen roughly $250K from Bishop. Not a huge sum, and no individual transaction is over $500. It has been just enough to pad her meager salary, buy a sexy sports car, and stay under the radar. I wonder how much more she needs before she can start going to a hair salon and upgrade her wardrobe, but maybe that is intentional, part of her disguise.

I look up some of the invoices in our electronic storage, and it is easy to figure out how she did it. With the help of software, Mazie created realistic invoices on which she forged approval signatures. She most likely had plenty of examples of what the signatures were supposed to look like, since the vendor setup forms must have come to her.

After she forged the approval, she coded the invoices to different cost centers so as not to overly burden any one in particular. No manager is going to take the time to chase down a $500 utility charge, and no accounts payable clerk bothers to scrutinize such familiar vendors. She probably came in early to put her invoices into the Cash Disbursement department basket, then changed the payment instructions in the system to her own bank account.

After the checks processed, she changed the remittance address back to the proper one so AT&T never needed to inquire about a missed payment. This cycle continued week after week, and as far as I can tell, no one but me has any idea it is going on. The fraud is a fairly common type, and all auditors worth their salt could recognize the scheme if they looked at the activity for existing vendors—which any competently designed test would have required.

Yet the program Frank designed only reviews new vendors and not the changes to existing ones, so doing the test as instructed would not reveal this particular fraud. And Frank was noncommittal when I asked him about doing the extra testing that has revealed it.

So should I mention it to Frank or not? After Monday's meeting, I am feeling a little gun-shy as far as my professional judgment is concerned. Nonetheless, I recall hearing once that curiosity is one of the most valuable traits in an auditor, and I definitely have that trait in spades.

Just to be sure, I conduct the test as instructed, with just the new vendors, and save the work papers and the shared drive file. Test complete with no exceptions noted.

Now I need to give some thought about the best way to inform Frank of my findings. I imagine a few scenarios. "Gee, Frank," I could simper, "I'm confused about the activity in the vendor account. It seems awfully high to me. What do you think I should do?" Or I could call in an anonymous tip, or I could write a letter to the Chief Compliance Officer. I elect to do none of those things. After all, fraud is fraud, and it is my job to bring such matters to my team. It is unthinkable that they would be against this in the same way they were against my charming my way onto the executive floor.

There is a big difference between expanding an audit test where there are clear indications of accounts payable fraud, and snooping in the executive medicine cabinet. There is absolutely no embarrassment for the department with the former. Plus, uncovering fraud makes internal auditors seem valuable to outsiders. If I go to Frank and expose Mazie's fraud, he, as someone who supervises me and my work, will share in the accolades from Hal and his supervisors.

Perhaps my discovery will put me back in his good graces, and I will be recognized after all and have some hope of upward mobility. Yes, this is my redeeming moment, I decide. This will erase yesterday's debacle and not just restore but also enhance my value to the team. I envision Hal and Frank beaming, Moe and Frank arguing about who gets to use me on their assignments, and Hal settling it all by giving me my own audits. "Tanzie, let's see what you can do with trading derivatives."

I am having trouble containing myself, but then I see the three of them returning, toothpicks busily dislodging bits of lunch from their teeth as they walk right by me and close Hal's door behind them.

While the three of them are meeting, I take the opportunity to pay a visit to my new parking lot friend, who according to the company directory has an office on the ninth floor. I don't want to confront her, just see where she sits and get a feel for her surroundings. I walk around the ninth floor and finally spy her nameplate outside an interior cube.

She is not at her desk when I poke my head inside her area. Her cube is fairly standard, with a wire basket for incoming requests just to the right of her computer monitor. There are magnetic crosses affixed to the cabinet doors above her workstation and a framed award from her church for her tireless efforts for the annual spring fundraiser, from which, I have no doubt, she skimmed some of the proceeds. I do wonder if she tithes the standard 10 percent of her takings.

Mazie must still be at lunch because her computer screen saver is on, indicating she's been gone awhile. Three toddlers, dressed alike, stare up at me. *Must be her grandchildren*, I think. *I wonder if I would be a grandmother by now, if Winston and I had decided to have kids.*

When we first discussed marriage, I wanted a large family and was disappointed that Winston did not. *Big money would have made child rearing much easier than it had been for my parents*, I think. Winston wanted no children, pointing out that he traveled frequently and didn't feel as though he would make a good father, being so obsessed with succeeding in business.

Winston had been an only child, and although he had liked my siblings and all the little nieces and nephews, he had absolutely no desire to complicate his life with his own offspring. In the negotiations on the question of kids, I had caved and had justified the decision by taking great vacations and accompanying Winston on his frequent trips to New York and London.

As the years went by, his invitations for my companionship had grown more infrequent, so I had filled the gap by perfecting my golf game and spending time at our club. Our dog, a black Labrador retriever we named Rocky, had become the focus of our parental inclinations. We had become one of *those* couples, with pets instead of children.

My God, I am old, I'm thinking as I look at Mazie's grandbabies, as they are often referred to in Oklahoma. I decide to leave before more depressing thoughts enter my brain, and I head back to my floor. I take the stairs rather than the elevator this time.

I'm fat, old, and out of shape, I think as I march down the stairs to my cube on six. *I need to start exercising and get a facelift.* These same thoughts had consumed me in the months after my divorce. It is so like women to blame themselves for the despicable behavior of their men. If only I had kept myself up, if only I was better at whatever . . . For me, those thoughts quickly gave way to placing the blame squarely where it belonged, especially when I recalled the last time I saw Winston.

I remember being in my lawyer Stu Van Dyke's office for about the sixth or seventh settlement discussion.

"This valuation is bullshit and you know it, Winston." I looked across the table as my husband and his lawyer Rick exchanged "not this again" looks.

"And what about our working interest in those wells in North Dakota? And the deferred comp plan? Your compensation is a matter of public record. I have the proxy right here in my purse." I got up to leave. My lawyer stayed seated, intimidated for the moment by my ability to find what he had not. "This is so ridiculous," I continued as I walked to the door. "I do our tax return, remember?" It had occurred to me early into the divorce proceedings that divorce lawyers are not financial experts, and my background was actually stronger at the nuts and bolts of transactions than Winston's or either of our attorneys'. Despite his Rice MBA, Winston resided in the world of structured deals and high finance rather than the transactional minutia in which I, as a CPA, was an expert. Still, the mistakes I pointed out were too large to have been oversights.

"Please sit down, Mrs. Lewis. Please." Rick stood up and gestured to my chair. "Give us a minute to get our ducks in a row here."

"Look, Winston. Just play fair and we can get this over with. I don't want the house! The yard! The putting green! The pool! How am I supposed to maintain all of that? I haven't worked since Bush Senior was in office, for God's sake." I had known women who had made that rookie mistake, opting to keep their stylish residences only to have to sell when they could not manage the upkeep on a barista's minimum wage. "And you, sir," I pointed at Rick, "have had ample time to align your ducks!"

"Stu, can you please try to get your client under control?" Rick appealed, lawyer to lawyer.

"Good luck," Winston snickered as he leaned sideways in his chair so he could cross his legs. The bottom buttons of his shirt were straining to stay fastened as he unbuttoned his blazer. I could tell he was losing patience with the whole process. He glanced at his watch the way busy people do when they are looking at a packed schedule.

"Can we please move this along?" Winston said, taking the reins. "What is it you want, Tanzie? There might be some errors in the documents, just tell us what's missing and we'll fix it. No one's trying to cheat you. Honestly."

"Forgive me if I don't believe these are honest mistakes. You haven't been honest with me about a lot of things—"

"Here we go again," Winston interrupted. "You had it pretty good, Tanzie—golf, shopping, travel. You'll wind up with a decent settlement and I have no doubt you'll find some sort of job. You're a CPA; the judge agreed you wouldn't require spousal support after the divorce is final."

"My license isn't current, Winston. You know that."

"Mrs. Lewis. Mrs. Lewis. Please. We're getting off

track." Stu tapped the tip of his pen on the table to get my attention. "Let's get back to the settlement offer."

"What offer? This is incomplete. I won't agree to this." I shoved the paper across to Rick and Winston's side of the table. "I have no job and this man wants me to take the house and all that upkeep? He conveniently leaves out assets. Why am I the bad guy here? *You* left *me*, Winston." I tried to hold back the tears but my eyes watered up anyway.

"Don't make me feel guilty about wanting something more in my life," he grumbled. I watched as he grabbed the flab under his chin; a habit he had when he became irritated.

Of course not, Winston, we wouldn't want you *to feel guilty.* I stared at the balding toad across the table and marveled at his gall. I sat back down and took the proxy out of my purse, pretending to reconcile the compensation information to what was on Rick's settlement offer. My mind was in another place, though, and I rested my forehead on my hand as I looked down at the documents and then up at Winston, wondering why my life was falling apart.

I thought back to when we first met, when he was the CFO for a client of mine in the early '80s. Winston was very handsome back then, and I fell very hard very quickly. He was charmed by my bohemian upbringing on the West Coast and my eccentric family. Winston had grown up with strict boundaries in a disciplined WASP home, and I suppose he felt a bit of liberation hanging around the O'Learys. I would never forget our first trip to San Francisco while we were dating. He was sitting at the Formica kitchen table when one of my sisters, Bumby, I think, handed him a baby to hold while she tended to some other task. I don't think Winston had ever held a child before. Baby Molly unexpectedly reached up and hit Winston's arm, sending a nearly full glass of red wine flying across the kitchen.

Now if that had happened in Winston's family, there would have been an immediate damage assessment and discussion about who was to blame for the accident. In mine, however, my mother called out, "Tanzie, get this boy some more wine! His glass is empty." The horrified look on Winston's face dissolved into laughter. The O'Leary home must have been a welcome relief from the stress Winston was used to. No judgments. Just acceptance. I think Winston was drawn to that at that time of his life. By the end of the evening he was singing "Goodnight, Irene" with Bumby's husband Shamus. He proposed to me on the flight back to Houston.

"I want it all liquidated." I looked up at Winston. "We'll split it all down the middle. We can divvy up the securities to save on taxes, but the house, the place in Santa Fe, and the condo in Cayman and all the contents, I want sold. I'm not going to burn up money maintaining those properties in a down market. Who knows when this recession will turn around?"

"That's shortsighted, Tanzie. Selling in this market is lunacy; everything's under water!" Winston shouted. This was unusual for him, and I knew I had his attention.

"You asked me what I wanted and that's what I want."

Winston collected himself and raised his eyebrows while he shook his head. Silence and then more silence while he stared at the table in disbelief. He then raised his head. "Do it, Rick. Just do it."

Now Winston was the one getting up to leave.

"Just one more thing, Mr. Lewis," Stu said. "We haven't agreed on who should take the dog, Rocky."

Winston and I looked at each other. "He's my dog, Tanzie. You gave him to me for Christmas. Doesn't that mean he's mine?" Winston looked at Rick and then Stu.

"I suppose so, Mr. Lewis," Stu answered. "It would appear that the dog would be considered your separate property, but my understanding is that he is currently living with Mrs. Lewis."

"Well, he can continue to until the house sells, and then he'll come with me. No sense making him live in an apartment downtown."

"Winston, can't we share him? He spends more time with me . . . I trained him. You can take him hunting, but—"

"I've had enough for one day! You're selling our assets in the worst market since '29. A ridiculous move, in my opinion. Rocky is my dog. End of story, Tanzie."

Winston made his exit, and Rick gathered his papers

and hurried after him. I heard the elevator ding and stared at Stu, who was making himself look useful by poring over the proxy statement he had no ability to comprehend. Winston was right about selling in a down market, but it was the only way I had left to hurt him. I was the suicide bomber of our combined wealth. I took a cigarette out of my purse and began to light up.

"Mrs. Lewis, I'm afraid there's no smoking allowed."

I took a drag and stubbed it out on the settlement folder left behind by Rick. I gathered my things and left without another word.

During my divorce proceedings, the women at the club suggested I invest in myself: A month at La Costa, a facelift, strategic lipo, a little nip and tuck. Several of my friends had used a particular plastic surgeon in Atlanta who for $40K would restore a natural and youthful appearance to your face. The fee included private nursing at a five-star hotel in which you could stay until your scars looked more like an automobile accident than vanity. Tempting as that was, I was nervous about being off the gravy train of a steady and high income. Texas does not provide for alimony, so the settlement was it for me, and I didn't want to risk depleting my savings too quickly.

There is no way with my entry-level salary at Bishop that I will be flying to Atlanta or San Diego anytime soon. But maybe, if I play my cards right with this fraud and get a promotion, I can feel better about putting a dent in the portfolio—only, of course, *after* I write NYU a check for Lulu's tuition.

When I return to my floor, the three are still behind closed doors, so I am once again relegated to sitting tight for an indefinite period, until I notice the red light on my phone indicating I have a message. It is from my friend Beth, a recipient of one of those $40K procedures. Her message says she has been trying to reach me all morning on my cell but it just goes to voice mail, and she sounds frustrated. She says she's sorry to call me at work and asks me to call her right away. I can tell by her voice that this isn't a social call. I fish in my purse and plug my dead phone into the charger before calling her back on the office line, ignoring potential exposure to my cube neighbors. I reach Beth and she is in her car driving on the freeway.

"I have terrible news, Tanzie," she says.

"Oh no, Beth, what is it? Is Grant okay?"

"He's fine. I don't know if you heard," she continues. "Ken and Alice were killed in the explosion this morning. The kids too. They were visiting for Easter and stayed a couple of extra days."

My heart sinks and I feel the tears burn down my cheeks. "But they don't live anywhere near there," I say, voice shaking. "What were they doing in the Galleria?"

"They sold their place in Memorial in January and bought one of those new condos. Downsizing since the boys were off at SMU."

"Oh, Matt and Eric. I can't believe it."

"It's so terrible . . . we felt the explosion this morning all the way out at our house. Everyone is in shock. The flames just incinerated that whole block. They're saying fifty-two people are confirmed dead and countless more injured. That seems low when you look at all the housing in that area . . ."

I am finding it hard to talk. Not only is there a lack of privacy, but also I am crying so hard that I can't get words out effectively.

"There's going to be a service this Friday and I wanted to make sure you knew," Beth says.

I retrieve an old tissue from my purse and blow my nose while covering the phone mouthpiece, trying to compose myself.

"Of course, I'll come down. I'll book a flight as soon as I get off the phone."

"You'll stay with us, okay? I miss you . . . you never call. It'll be good to see you again, Tanzie."

"All right. Thanks Beth, I'll call you with the details when I get everything taken care of. Give my best to Grant."

I hang up the phone and cradle my head in my hands. I am too shocked to think straight, but I know I need to get out of the office. I draft an email to Hal, Frank, and Moe indicating that I am not feeling well and am going home, then shut off my computer and head for the elevator. My eyes sting under my dark designer sunglasses, and I try not to bawl publicly as I walk to the garage. As I drive to the exit, I pass Mazie's red Mercedes.

CHAPTER SIX

Once home, I pour a stiff scotch instead of the usual white wine and go to my balcony for a smoke. I had forgotten all about the explosion when I discovered the fraud, and then forgotten all about the fraud when I heard about the Mayhews. Suddenly, I do not care about who is ripping off Bishop or where my career is going or not going.

Why couldn't I have called Alice or e-mailed or joined Facebook? Some horrible part of me must have wanted to punish her, I suppose. Why? For having a husband who adored her? For having children when I hadn't? Had I really expected her to pick sides and not allow Ken to socialize with his best friend? The truth is that I was embarrassed that I worked out of a cube and couldn't keep up financially with my old lifestyle. I'm sure Alice hadn't cared, but I did. I had let jealousy and pride skew my better judgment. I knew then that I needed to make plans to get back to Houston and reconnect with the friends I had left.

———◆———

I awake a little dehydrated, and my eyes are so puffy that even cucumber and Preparation H do not help. "Female problems," I write in the e-mail, which assures me that neither Hal nor Moe and Frank will want any elaboration. As a new employee, I have not accrued time off, but they can take it out of my check; it amounts to all of $500, give or take.

I make a few calls, buy a ticket, and by 10:00 a.m. I'm on a tiny commuter plane headed for Houston. I could have easily leveled with Hal, and I am certain he would have given me the time off without pay, but I didn't want to broadcast the connection between the Bishop explosion and my friends' untimely deaths around the company. It seems too private to share with anyone in Tulsa just yet, particularly Hal, Moe, or Frank.

At the airport, I rent a silver beer can of a car for $26 a day and head south on Highway 59 toward the Houston skyline. Although Beth has insisted that I stay with her, I did win the point about having my own car, probably so I won't need to interrupt her Wednesday morning golf to pick me up at the airport. I am a little surprised that Beth is on the golf course so soon after such a tragedy, but I suppose that's how she is choosing to cope with her grief—just by continuing with her routine.

I arrive at her River Oaks home while she is still at the club and am greeted at the door by Maria, her housekeeper of twenty-five years who lives in the quarters above the garage. Maria gives me a hug and a smile and takes one of my bags. I follow her upstairs to the guest bedroom, where she leaves me to freshen up after the flight. Sadly, there isn't much to freshen. A gilded mirror hangs by the bed, and I cringe at my reflection as I walk by. I wish I'd had more notice before re-encountering my swank social set. I have gained about twenty-five pounds and my hair, though better than Mazie's, has suffered under the care of the Tulsa salons I've been using, trying to save a buck. It has been a tough six months for me, and it shows in my budding turkey neck and crow's feet. I am starting to get that dumpy old lady look that will relegate me to stretchy jogging suits and oversized blouses, which is a difficult trend to reverse once it sets in. I turn away from the mirror and head downstairs, hoping to be spared from another view of my depressing reflection.

It is a beautiful spring day in Houston, so I sit in one of the cushioned patio chairs under an arbor by Beth's pool. Maria brings me a Diet Coke, and I am finishing a game of Bedazzled Blitz on my iPhone when I hear the French door open and see a smiling Beth reaching out for a hug. *Wow, she looks great*, I think: Sleeveless polo shirt and not a bit of arm fat wiggling. Her legs are tanned except for her ankles and feet, which are pasty white with bright pink toenails peeking out from Ferragamo sandals.

"It's so good to see you! I have really missed you, Tanzie."

She sits down and lights up a cigarette, offers me one, which I accept—when in Rome—and then I listen while Beth fills me in on the details of the explosion. We reminisce about Alice and the Wednesday mornings we'd spent out at Ravenswood together. We cry and then cry some more. As we light up a third cigarette, Beth shifts the conversation, giving me an update on what's going on at the club.

"Sandy and Van just got back from their place in Carmel last week, and Grant and I are thinking of going with them to Scotland in May. You know, St. Andrews, Royal Dornoch, Muirfield, that whole thing. Grant's a little on the fence, though. I'm not sure he can take Van in large quantities; he can be bit overbearing. We're seeing if we can get another couple to go with us—"

Beth catches herself. She knows full well that the other couple would have been Winston and me a few years ago.

Maria breaks the tension by appearing with a couple of salads with grilled chicken and fat-free dressing for lunch. Beth is a low-carb, low-fat gal, and I cannot argue with the results. Maybe I will lose a pound or two staying here for the next couple of days.

I can tell Beth is a little surprised by how awful I look, and she jumps at the chance to pull some strings and get me into her salon for a quick makeover. "Rachel is a miracle worker, Tanzie. She says she can fit you in if you get over there right away."

"I'm certainly in need of a miracle. Can she do something about this?" I joke, wiggling some excess skin around my neck.

"No, but I know someone in Atlanta who can." Beth smiles and I smile back, grabbing my purse and fishing out the gigantic rental car key chain.

I head out for my cut and color, promising to be back in time to join Beth and Grant for dinner. Despite my deep sorrow for Alice and Ken, it feels good to be home again, and I drive to the salon noticing all the changes that have happened in Houston during the six months I have been gone. Houston has no zoning, so wealthy neighborhoods abut ganglands, and high-rise office towers have sprouted right in the middle of residential areas. I remember the uproar from a number of years ago when the forty-story Marathon Oil building destroyed the privacy of the Tanglewood gentry who could no longer skinny-dip in their swimming pools without being seen by teams of petroleum engineers.

In the short time I have been in Tulsa, luxury high- and mid-rise condos have also sprung up from the West Loop all the way east to downtown, like mushrooms after a rainstorm. The salon is over by the Galleria, and the traffic on the main artery is diverted because of the explosion. I am shocked by the devastation as I pass slowly by in the stop-and-go traffic that's typical of this area, even on a good day. I am not that close to the explosion site, but the ground is still smoldering and the rubble from the fifteen-story condo building has taken out windows and dented cars for more than half a mile in every direction. I cry all over again and watch tears blackened with mascara flecks drip onto my lap.

When I get to the salon, Rachel is running behind, and I take the opportunity to go next door to Win Win, a dress shop I had frequented over the years. Its flaming owner, Tommy Nguyen, recognizes me instantly and comes running over with his arms open.

"You look horrible, Mrs. Lewis," he chastises. "I haven't seen you in months."

"Thanks," I say. "I moved to Tulsa."

"Whatever for?" he asks.

"It's a long story, Tommy. I'm down here staying with Beth McAfee. Did you know Alice Mayhew was killed in the explosion? She's shopped here a few times."

Tommy lets out a gasp and covers his mouth.

"Her husband and children, too. It's just the worst," I say, shaking my head. I decide to change the subject to avoid another bout of crying. "I'm getting my hair done next door. I only have a few minutes and I know I look terrible. Any chance you can find something for me to wear?"

Tommy gives me a long hug. Once he releases me he steps back, giving me a head-to-toe review. "You have gained weight," he says, all business. "Shame on you. But I think we can make you look good, Mrs. Lewis."

Tommy grabs some items from the racks and calls for his brother Danny, who does the alterations.

I try on a black dress and Danny gets busy with the pins; the Ungaro slacks and blazer are next. I am horrified to see the European equivalent of a size 14 tag on the pants and even more horrified that the waistband needs to be let out a tad. "This is all I can do today," Danny says, and he bustles out of the room.

I change back into my things, leave a credit card with Tommy, and walk back to the salon. Within minutes I am getting my nails done while I sit with folded foil packets all over my head. Rachel does indeed deliver a miracle, and just after 6 p.m. I walk out, not a new woman, but my old self plus a few pounds. Win Win is officially closed for the evening, but Tommy opens up for me and I go into the dressing room, emerging moments later in slacks and a blazer that fit perfectly. I give Tommy a kiss on the cheek and thank him for his kindness.

As I sit in the car, I realize how far I have fallen from my old life and shake my head, wondering if I will ever get it back.

I give Beth a call, and we agree to meet at the Grotto, my favorite Italian restaurant. By the time I make it to the restaurant, Beth and Grant are already seated and wave at me to come over when I enter through the bar. Grant gives me a kiss on the cheek.

"You look great!" he lies.

"You too." I smile.

We order drinks and the discussion turns to the explosion. Grant knows I work for Bishop and treads gingerly so he doesn't offend me with his disgust over the tragedy.

"No one is sure why it happened," he concludes. "May have been some digging. There certainly is a lot of construction going on in that area."

"Or it could have been their fault," I say. "They have a culture of cutting corners. I wouldn't be surprised to find out they used substandard piping or didn't maintain the system properly. They seem—"

"Not a very loyal employee, are we?" Beth interrupts.

"Not these days." I take a breadstick out of the basket, knowing I will be the only one consuming carbs tonight. It seems like the better choice over the garlic bread and focaccia. Still, Beth raises her eyebrow, so I put it down on my bread plate after taking a single bite.

"Bill Matheson is handling some of the lawsuits," Grant says. "I know Alice's parents have retained him. There may be others as well."

"That's right up his alley. He'll do a good job," I say, eyeing the breadstick.

"Bill's already been interviewed on the news a few times." Beth leans toward me and lowers her voice. "He's such an obnoxious blowhard. I don't know how Julie puts up with him."

"That's what makes him such a good lawyer, Beth," Grant says, defending his pal.

"True," I say. "But I'll never know how all of you last for eighteen holes listening to all his baloney."

"We've been friends so long, I probably just don't notice it," Grant says with a shrug. "Man, you girls are mean."

Beth and I look at each other and smile. It was no secret that we didn't like Bill and Julie. "I think I've uncovered a fraud," I say, changing the topic. I give them the particulars of the Mazie caper, including the sports car and dowdy appearance.

"What are you going to do about it?" Beth asks. "Prosecute?"

"Not sure. I tried to tell my boss but I just haven't had a chance," I answer.

Grant is an insurance executive and begins a tale he heard about from a colleague.

"You know, years ago, my buddy over at Marsh was asked to cover a claim on a fraud down in Brazil. One of the major oil companies, not sure which one, had a posh office down there. In the president's office hung a very expensive oil painting, a Mark Rothko, I think. During the collapse of oil prices in the mid-'80s, the office was closed, and when the painting was appraised for shipment back to the States, they discovered it was a forgery."

"Oh no! Did they know who stole the real one?" I ask with a smile.

"They thought, but could not prove, that sometime during her employment the president's secretary had substituted the original with a copy, and no one had noticed."

"Can you imagine? This woman, who probably loved art, working for this Jethro who would have preferred dogs playing poker or a velvet Elvis." Beth laughs.

"You have no idea what it is like to work for people like that," I chime in. "I'd probably do the same thing, if I'd been clever enough to think of it."

"The best crimes are the ones where no one can figure out who done 'em," Grant concludes, and we all laugh.

"I went to a continuing education seminar on fraud awhile back," I say. "The instructor referred to a 'fraud triangle' to explain the factors that cause someone to commit a fraud. The theory is that there must be pressure, opportunity, and the ability to rationalize the act. This guy took it one step further. He thought everyone had the potential to commit a fraud; the tipping point is unique to each person. It's in every one of us, though."

Beth takes exception to this idea. "I would never steal!"

"Not even if you were starving to death or your child was starving? You wouldn't steal a piece of bread? Didn't you see *Les Misérabes*?"

"Well, maybe. But that's different!"

It isn't different, though. It is just a matter of degree. Beth and Grant have so much money that they would never feel the pressure to steal, because they can always buy what they need.

"The same triangle can apply to unethical behavior other than stealing—such as cheating on your wife," I say. "Pressure: You really need to get laid; opportunity: A beautiful babe is interested in you, a potbellied, rich old fart; rationalization: Your wife is sick, bored, disgusted by you, or all of the above."

"I do not have a potbelly!" Grant says grinning.

"I was talking about Winston," I say.

They get quiet. "Have you talked to Winston lately?" Beth asks.

When I say no, Beth and Grant exchange looks.

"Caroline is pregnant. Did you know?" Beth finally says.

I down the rest of my martini and signal the waiter to bring me another.

"Oh my," I muster. "Is that a good thing?"

Grant and Beth decide not to answer my question, and we are saved by the waiter bringing our entrées to the table. Suddenly, I wish I had ordered the lasagna instead of having what Beth ordered: the broiled fish and steamed spinach, all taste on the side. Impulsively, I take a piece of garlic bread from the basket and consume it in a single bite, issuing Beth a "don't judge me" look as I reach for another.

"How would you steal the painting?" Grant asks to break the silence.

"What?"

"You said you would probably do the same thing. How would you go about it?"

Grant is a sweetheart for trying to take my mind off Winston.

"I don't know. Probably take a picture of the real one, have a forgery made, and then switch them over a weekend or after hours."

"It's a huge painting. You don't think security would see you?"

"Let me tell you a thing or two about building security." I begin the tale of my Easter Sunday, assuring them that you could probably convince the security guard to hang the fake painting for you and load the priceless one into your car, all without the slightest inquiry as to what you are doing.

"It always amazes me that businesses tend to leave something so critical under the control of minimum wage rent-a-cops."

We finish our dinner refining criminal strategies. I am grateful for the temporary diversion.

———◆———

When we return to the house, Beth and Grant leave me while I head out to the patio for a nightcap and to chain-smoke the last five cigarettes in my pack. I think of Winston raising a child at his age. I guess now that his climb to the top is finally complete, he can devote himself to fatherhood with a new young wife. How lucky for him, I decide, and I smoke and sob quietly, thinking about Winston starting a family and me not even having my dog.

CHAPTER SEVEN

When I wake, I find the house empty. Groggily, I walk through silence and unfamiliar rooms until I come across Beth on the patio, a newspaper spread out on a glass table in front of her and a lit cigarette in her hand. Maria brings out some coffee and fruit for me, and I bum a cigarette from Beth. I had smoked all mine the night before. I grimace as I look down at the *Houston Chronicle*. News of the pipeline explosion dominates every story on the front page.

"At least there's a nice obituary for Alice and Ken," Beth says. She folds the paper back to an interior page and hands it to me. "I can't believe they're gone."

I take the paper and look down at the low-resolution, gray-toned picture of Alice and Ken. It isn't their best; Alice's makeup was smudged under her left eye and Ken was smiling too broadly the way he sometimes did after a few drinks. It gave him a whole extra chin. Alice's mother must have had to choose one where their faces were close together so that it could be cropped to fit the copy. There are too many gray squares of faces crowding that page. I put the paper back down.

"I can't read it now. It's like if I think about it too much I'll just start crying and never stop."

"I know. Me too."

"I hope Bill burns that company to the ground, just sues the living shit out them," I say finally. Beth purses her lips and nods, tearing up a bit.

"You'd be out of a job."

I nod. "I've had enough of Tulsa and enough of that stupid job. It's like stepping back in time every morning." I give Beth a recap of the work situation—every single misstep and reprimand. Office politics are lost on Beth, but when I am done, she hugs me and pats my back.

"You can always come back. You can join Ravenswood," she suggests. "Margie is the worst tournament partner I've ever had. She can't sink a putt and it's killing me." She stutters through those last words as she tries to catch her breath after all the crying.

"Beth, I'm a weekend golfer at best," I say. "Besides, I'm fifty-two. I need a job that comes with health insurance. It's a lousy market right now, especially for someone my age. I'm lucky to have anything. I'll keep looking for something down here, but for now I'm stuck where I am."

"Don't be so down on yourself, Tanzie. You just need to get back on your feet."

"Thanks," I say, shrug, and look out beyond the patio. I don't want to continue the conversation. What is friendly reassurance going to do to fix this situation, any of it? Maybe I can get back on my feet in a few years, but I am never going to be a country club regular again. Beth cannot understand it. My charmed life is over, while Beth's is only just hitting its stride. I have been cut from that team with no hope of returning.

Beth excuses herself to get dressed and then run some errands. There is a visitation for Ken, Alice, and the boys that evening, and we are planning a late dinner out afterward. Beth tells me she will be out of pocket most of the day since one of the charity boards she volunteers on is planning a gala that's scheduled in a few weeks. That is fine with me. Relaxing at their River Oaks estate is like vacationing at a five-star resort, something that is beyond my reach at the moment.

I experience some guilt for feeling sorry for myself when I start to read the article about Ken and Alice. What do I have to complain about? Still, I am surprised to read in the second paragraph that Ken had graduated from the University of Kansas in the late '70s and had played on the Jayhawk football team. The word "Jayhawk" sounds familiar, and then I remember the password under Marla's pen set.

I call to Beth upstairs and ask if I can borrow a computer.

"Grant has one in his office," she yells back. "Feel free."

Bishop does not allow telecommuting but does have remote access so that employees can work from home after hours, on weekends, or while traveling. I access the login site, https://portal.bishopgroup.com. I type BBISHOP as the user name and then look at the saved memo on my iPhone and type GOJayhawks!17 as the password. *Access denied* flashes back at me. With two BBISHOPs, I figure maybe one of their user IDs includes a middle initial. Baldwin's is *R* for Robert and Bennet's is *C* for Charles. BRBISHOP, I type, and boom, I'm in. I am looking at a Citrix screen with subheadings for web bookmarks, secured folders, and terminal sessions. The screen displays *Welcome to Bishop secure access, BRBishop.*

I quickly log out. I am shaking. Why did I just do that? What if they trace the login to Grant? I do not want to involve him. Also, what if Baldwin was on his computer when I accessed it? Would he be able to tell I was in there, too?

I need some time to think about what to do with this access. I initially thought the Jayhawk password was Marla's, but Baldwin probably gave her access so she could send email on his behalf. Clearly it would be interesting to eavesdrop during this explosion crisis; I just don't want to get arrested doing it.

"Get what you needed?" Beth asks, stopping by Grant's office.

"Oh yes. Thanks."

"See ya this evening." And with that, I hear Beth's footsteps headed down the hallway and the heavy door to the garage shut loudly.

I start to get up and notice a flash drive sticking out of Grant's computer. I remember the one in my purse that has the files I took from Marla's desktop. I run upstairs to get my purse, and in seconds I have replaced Grant's portable device with my own. I have an overwhelming desire to spy on Baldwin. I want to know what he knew about the explosion that incinerated my friends and their children. I do not feel comfortable logging on to his computer while there is a chance he might be on it, but I can gain some familiarity by checking out the files I downloaded on Easter. Maybe the files will be as dull as his medicine cabinet, but I won't know if I don't look. Perhaps they will provide some insight that will help me later on.

I click on the first folder, titled "LEAR," and open one of the documents in the 2010 subfolder. There are seven or eight documents, all headed the same: Large Expenditure Authorization Request. Each document is a proposal from a business segment to spend a large amount of money on a project. There are financial models and return on investment rates along with supporting spreadsheets and narratives describing the benefits, risks, and other details associated with each proposal. Approved proposals have either Bennet's or Baldwin's signature on the bottom of the PDF file. Denied or deferred proposals have that status indicated on the signature line.

This is pretty interesting stuff, and it makes me forget that I am a nobody with a career going nowhere. By noon I have made it through 2010. I enjoy reading about each project and looking at the numbers supporting the request. I chuckle to myself when I notice that an approved project to build a gas plant in Kansas has a bust in the spreadsheet calculating the return on investment. Based on my calculation, the return should be closer to 3 percent than the 9 percent appearing in the request. I wonder if they will ever figure that out when the actual numbers come in.

Maria comes by to see if I want lunch, but I am too engrossed in my reading to stop. Around 4:00 I finish with 2009 and open the 2008 folder. Scanning the titles I notice a file named LEAR_2008_17_Houston_Gas and open that one up first. After starting on the narrative part of the form, I slowly put my hand to my mouth as I read.

This proposal is for a large-scale maintenance project for a gas pipeline in Houston. According to the proposal, the pipeline dates back to the 1930s and extends from West Texas to a hub near the Gulf Coast. When it was originally built, it ran through what was considered the outskirts of Houston, but with the expansion over the last seventy-five years, it now has sections running through some heavily populated areas. The request references a report from Wagner Jones, Bishop's former Vice President of Environmental Health and Safety, or EH&S as it is generally referred to, indicating that corrosion had been identified during pigging of another section of the line and that there could very well be something similar in the section under the Houston property.

Pigging is a pipeline term that has nothing to do with real pigs, or quirky sayings by Mark Twain. A pig is an object that is run through the pipe to collect information about the integrity of the pipe, as well as to identify obstructions or other problems that could affect performance. The initial studies about potential corrosion on the Houston pipeline were inconclusive, however, and according to the accompanying report, the pipe would have to be excavated and examined to be absolutely certain.

The records are not complete, but it seemed to the engineers that the section of pipe running under the Galleria area was slightly larger and of a different spec than the other sections. No one could explain this, but it was not uncommon back in the day to use leftover materials from another project to save a dollar or two. The size change made the pigging results unreliable, and without physical inspection the engineers could not be certain as to the condition of the pipe.

But in order to do a physical inspection, housing on top of the pipe would need to be moved or raised onto pilings to allow for excavation. Further complicating the effort, Bishop could not find the maps indicating exactly where the pipes were. They had a general idea, but could only estimate within a forty-foot range.

The LEAR file includes e-mail correspondence between the Bishop brothers, Pipeline Integrity, Operations, and the environmental team trying to get their arms around what exactly the problems are and what to do about them. There is a worst-case scenario calculation that, to my horror, estimates the dollar value of each life potentially lost that could be netted for insurance recoveries should an explosion occur. Unfortunately, that figure, though in the millions, is far less than the excavation and replacement cost of that section of the pipe.

It appears that the Bishops didn't want to launch such a huge project on just a perceived risk rather than conclusive evidence, so they decided to defer the project and do more studies. Wagner was put in charge of coordinating with the Pipeline Integrity folks and Gas Operations and getting back to the executive team with more proposals.

Anyone who knows anything about Houston knows the rapid pace of change within the housing market. The lack of city zoning enables neighborhoods to change with astonishing frequency. Slums become haute and the other way around within just a few years. Such is the case in the Galleria area. When this LEAR was presented, the area was transitioning from rundown to upscale. The 1950s houses primarily used as rental property were being replaced by McMansions, million-dollar townhouses, and mid-rise condo buildings, including the one that was home to the Mayhews.

The initial loss calculations from the report were significantly undervalued and had not considered the recent gentrification of that particular section of the city. Even so, I am horrified that the company I work for had made a purely economic decision that had risked the safety of a community. What was the break-even point in human lives that would have compelled Bishop to take steps to find and maintain the pipeline? I wonder if they would have approved the LEAR if the loss calculation had been based on country club members versus immigrant families like the O'Learys.

I nearly jump out of my skin as Grant walks in, home from work early to get ready for the wake.

"Oh my God, you scared me!" I say, startled.

"I live here," he says, joking. "What's wrong, Tanzie? You look upset."

As much as I would love to tell Grant what I have just found, I decide to keep it to myself for the moment. I'm not sure how he would feel about me effectively stealing files.

"Oh, nothing, Grant," I lie. "Just catching up on paperwork."

I remove my flash drive and shut down his desktop, making sure I haven't saved anything to his computer. Then I go upstairs to shower and get ready. The whole time, I am shaking with anger. I now have proof of serious Bishop complicity in my friends' deaths.

———◆———

Normally, I would have been terribly stressed about seeing the old gang with so little time to prepare, but I am still too furious about the incriminating file to worry about my appearance. Besides, my black dress looks great thanks to Tommy, and I wonder how good a pregnant Caroline will look. I am hoping she looks as fat as a cow, with swollen ankles and sausage fingers.

Beth came home while I was getting ready and the three of us pile into Grant's Escalade for the ride to the funeral home.

The building is a tasteful combination of elegance and sterility—trimmed ivy covering ivory stucco with stern wrought iron accents. Gorgeous live oaks with white impatiens blooming underneath border a drive leading to the facility, and two huge porte cocheres extend outward to accommodate rows of limos in bad weather.

The parking lot is packed, but a valet is available to ease the congestion. Inside is crowded as well, and we stand in line for over fifteen minutes just to sign the guest book. This is not just any funeral home; it is Foster and Sons, the one that caters to the rich and famous of the Houston dead. They have remained independent rather than getting acquired by the funeral conglomerates and are known for their outstanding care during difficult times. In Houston, that means having a bar or two and catered hors d'oeuvres at all events.

Inside, a looping film on several flat screens shows photographs of the family from birth to their last Easter together less than a week ago. The caskets are closed, but there are large portraits of each individual, as well as a family one in black and white showing them on the beach in Galveston, all wearing jeans and white button-down shirts. I remember when Alice arranged for that sitting. I had helped her look through the proofs and select the very one on display. "You were such a great friend, and I've only been thinking of myself. I'm so sorry, Alice," I whisper as I touch her casket and reflect on how awful I have been.

I feel my eyes start to burn again as I stop to look at the picture of my sweet Matty. What a handsome young man he had become. Memories come flooding back between tears. Blubber-kissing him into hysteria as a toddler; chasing him around the backyard with his little brother Eric; caddying for him during the Jr. Club championship one year. Now I would never see how the story ended. What kind of girl he would fall in love with or what profession he would settle on. His life was slammed shut because cost projections were not finalized.

Guilt and then rage replaces my sorrow as I try to sort out my emotions. The disequilibrium sends me back to my childhood ritual in search of comfort, and I kneel by Matty's casket, making the sign of the cross. It has been years, but I remember the prayer my mother taught me growing up and that I had in turn taught Matt as part of my godmother duties.

"O, my God, I love Thee above all things, with my whole heart and soul, because Thou art all good and worthy of all love. I love my neighbor as myself for the love of Thee—"

I stop myself as I think of the next line of the prayer, "I forgive all who have injured me." Forgiveness is not a virtue I can embrace at the moment, so I leave it out of my casket-side vigil and go in search of something to help me compose myself and contemplate an appropriate revenge for my employer who regards my godson as nothing more than a number on a spreadsheet.

The line for the bar is mercifully short, and I have a glass of white wine in hand within minutes and survey the room. The wine feels good on my throat, raw from all the crying. I am surprised to see so many young people, but then I realize these must have been college and high school friends of the boys. Some of the faces seem familiar. Kids I'd seen at Alice's over the years. I am afraid of rekindling my emotional meltdown so I steer clear of Matt's friends.

As I snake through conversation circles, I see a group of ladies from the club and wander over to join in. Hugs and air kisses give way to more somber moments as we talk about how awful the explosion was and how sad it is that the whole family has been killed. I decide not to mention that I work for Bishop, and I manage any of my answers to questions related to Tulsa so as not to reveal that particular piece of information. I will let them hear it through the grapevine after I am long gone. As comforting as it is to see these women, I desperately want to get out of there and do more exploring of the Bishop files. It has been such a long time since anything has awakened my intellect, and I can tell I'm becoming obsessed with it. I wish I had driven my own car rather than be trapped at the funeral home.

Then I hear him: "Can I get you another drink, Cookie?" It is Winston from somewhere behind me, using his pet name for me.

My drink *is* almost empty; it is thoughtful of him, if inappropriate. I close my eyes and am just about to turn around to face him when I hear Caroline respond, "No, I'm just fine."

I take a deep breath and finally turn around. I am surprised by Winston's appearance. He is fit and tan and not at all like the pot-bellied, triple-chinned ape I had last seen at my lawyer's office. Caroline doesn't look pregnant at all. She is the same young, pretty thing who has replaced me in every aspect of my life, even Winston's pet name. Neither of them had seen me at all.

I have to get it over with; I walk over to greet them.

I catch Winston's eye and he nudges Caroline to exit from her current conversation with the wife of one of Ken's law partners. They smile at me the way winners often do when extending a consolation prize to the third runner-up.

"Glad you could come down," Winston says, and he introduces me to the new Mrs. Lewis.

After the divorce, I thought long and hard about changing my name back to O'Leary and had my attorney, Stu, put together the paperwork. I hated Winston and the thought of being confused with Caroline. Still, Tanzie Lewis had been the Ravenswood club champion; she had been the person who got a premier table at Houston's better restaurants and could get a call returned with a single message. People know who Tanzie Lewis is. *I* know who Tanzie Lewis is. I wasn't going to let Winston take one more thing from me. I sent the paperwork back to Stu unsigned.

I extend my hand and Caroline gives it a firm shake. I have seen pictures but have never met her before in person. She worked at Winston's company, but we had never attended events together.

Winston was fairly careful in managing this sort of situation. Caroline was not his first fling during our marriage. Winston was a legendary womanizer, and I had learned long ago just to look the other way. I had thought him far too fiscally practical to divide our assets over something as frivolous as another woman. I have often wondered if things would have been different if he had just waited a little longer before going public with this affair. Winston filed for divorce just months before the 2008 stock market crash and financial crisis wreaked havoc on our accumulated wealth.

"You're looking fit, Winston."

"CrossFit! It's amazing. Caroline got me hooked." There are no comments about my appearance, and I am happy to move the perfunctory conversation along.

"I understand congratulations are in order," I say with a smile. Years of country club socializing have made me a master of hiding true emotions. So instead of throwing the rest of my wine at the hussy, I make small talk and feign excitement over their expectant bundle of joy.

"Having a baby is saying 'yes' to the future," New Cookie says and grins at Winston.

"I'm sure it is. How wonderful for you," I say, suppressing a gag.

"Can you believe Caroline has only gained five pounds and she's already at twenty weeks?" Winston gives her an endearing squeeze.

Ouch. Pretty sad when at five months pregnant, the new girl has a better waistline than the old girl.

"I'm at the gym every day!" she brags. "I've started playing golf, too, although I don't know how much longer I can keep that up."

"She has a fantastic swing," Winston adds. "A real natural. Shot an eighty-two last week, and she's only been playing a few months. We're thinking of going to Scotland in May with some other couples."

Ouch again. "Wow, that is really great. Good for you," I say. *I hope you get smacked in the head by one of Winston's slices,* I think. I decide to change the subject to something I actually care about. "How's Rocky doing?"

"Oh, we had to give him away," Caroline says brightly, and I see Winston give her arm a pinch. "I read in my book that dogs can become very jealous of a new baby, and we didn't want to take a chance. You know what I mean. God, can you imagine?" She leans toward me like we are sorority sisters.

"Why didn't you ask me to take him, Winston?" I ask, backing away. "For crying out loud!" I have to stop myself because other people are turning to look in my direction.

"Bill Matheson took him," Winston stammers quickly. "Rocky still gets to go hunting, just like the old days. Relax,

Tanzie! Jeez." I see Winston give Caroline a "see what I'm talking about?" look, so I collect myself to keep from reinforcing any bitch references Winston may have fed her over the past couple of years. I don't want my bad behavior to make it easier for her to justify ruining my life.

"Lulu got into NYU, Winston. Isn't that terrific? She'll be in the theater program," I say, changing my tone. *Maybe he will ask about financing. It's a long shot, but worth bringing up*, I think. Caroline looks confused.

"I'll tell you what's terrific." Winston laughs. "Not having to put every single O'Leary through college. The forward curve of that cost savings is fairly steep!" Caroline joins Winston in the laugh and I smile politely although inside I'm longing to slap his smiling face. "Will you be joining us for dinner?" Winston asks.

It occurs to me that Winston and Caroline are being included in the after-visitation dinner festivities with Beth, Grant, and the rest of the club folk. I really want out now. I am not sure I can keep up my good manners any longer.

"You know, I came here with Grant and Beth," I begin, "but I am so overcome from the sadness of this tragedy that I think I'll pass and take a cab home."

"Whatever you think is best," Winston says.

"It is good to see you again, Winston, and best of luck to both of you."

The club ladies are gone. I look around to find Beth, but instead run into Leanne and Mason near one of the food stations next the fire exit.

"Oh Lord, is that you Tanzie?" Mason shouts. "I hardly recognized you, darling. You've plumped up just like a Ball Park frank!"

"Yes I have, Mason. It's all that gourmet food in Tulsa." I smile at a horrified Leanne.

"Have you seen your ex, Tanzie? Turned into quite a specimen with all that working out. And wow, that babe he's married to—"

"Mason, honey, will you please get me a refill?" Leanne interrupts.

"God, I'm so sorry, Tanzie," Leanne whispers as she watches Mason amble toward the bar. "He really is in another world these days. He doesn't know what he's saying most of the time."

"No problem, Leanne. It's really okay."

I couldn't fault poor Mason for stating what probably everyone else and even I was thinking.

"Oh my God, Tanzie, Mason's talking with Alice's sister; I need to get over there." And she's off, leaving me frowning at the paunch below the waistband of my black dress. I suck in my stomach, noticing only a slight improvement. I exhale in defeat and continue my search for Beth.

"I'm not feeling well. I think I'll take a pass on dinner and get a cab back to your place. Do you mind?" I ask when I finally find her.

"It's not because Grant asked Winston and Caroline to come along, is it? I told him not to."

"No," I lie. "I'm really tired and sad. I just don't think I would be good company for anyone."

"We'll miss you," she says. But I can tell Beth is relieved that I'm not going.

CHAPTER EIGHT

"Take me to the Internet café in the Heights," I tell the driver when I get into the cab. "Do you know where that is?"

"Of course," he says in a thick accent.

"Great. But stop at Beck's first." I am really starving. Eating Beth-food all day yesterday and then nothing today has really left me dying for something delicious, and a hamburger will be just the thing to sober me up and sustain me for a night of hacking into Baldwin Bishop's files. What are another couple thousand calories, after all?

I text Beth and tell her I've had a change of plans and not to wait up for me.

She texts back almost immediately. "OK. I'll leave the back patio door open and the alarm off."

It is 7:30 p.m. when the cab drops me off, and I ask him to return at 10:00. I had only heard about this particular place from others. In my lovely black dress, I look a bit formal for the place. It isn't really a café but an Internet bar where you can order a drink and sit at a terminal, paying for services with a credit card or a code from the cashier, if you prefer the anonymity of cash, as is the custom of most Nigerian princes. I choose the cash option; anonymity is going to be important for what I am doing. I skip the bar and enter my code into the access page.

The first thing I do is check my e-mail account since I have been out of the office a couple of days. I am not important enough to have been issued a company phone or Blackberry, and I had refused to have my private iPhone configured to get email. Thus the only way to access my work e-mail is to actually be at my desk or access it remotely. Clearly my role at Bishop is expendable, and there is nothing particularly urgent about any of my assignments.

I sift through the ten or so e-mails before reading one from Moe. He asks if I can attempt another security review over the weekend, only this time "use better judgment and stay off the executive floors." I am to look for unprotected passwords, confidential stuff in the trash cans, or unlocked office doors. There is another e-mail from Frank. He is sorry I am under the weather but wants to see if I can complete some testing by Monday. I write back that I am still quite ill and don't think I can make it in tomorrow, but tell him that if I feel better I will come in over the weekend to do it. There is no reason anything needs to be completed by Monday; it is purely a power trip on his part.

I turn my attention away from Frank and his nonsense, and within a minute or two I am logging in to Baldwin's account. I am fairly certain he is gone from the office by now, or if not, he is unlikely to be behind a computer. I click on the webmail icon and go immediately to his Outlook account.

I scroll through the inbox looking for the juiciest stuff but decide it will be better to adopt a more methodical approach. I read each e-mail, one by one, so as not to overlook anything. It is amazing what you can glean from reading a person's daily e-mail. The most current correspondence has to do with the Houston explosion, and I can also see from his calendar that there have been almost nonstop meetings with attorneys, insurance companies, and the environmental team since the explosion on Tuesday. I can also tell that Baldwin works from his iPhone starting around 6:00 each evening, so it is clear to me that I can roam around his desktop without detection after that time.

From his e-mail, it seems Baldwin is concerned about the families that perished in the disaster, but he is much more concerned with the impact on Bishop Group's bottom line. Several e-mails deal with revised estimates for damages and what will be covered and what will not. There is other correspondence asking if construction or sewer crews in the area could have caused the rupture. One e-mail from the attorneys suggests that Bishop quickly offer money to victims and thus contain civil damages. If the victims take initial cash, it may be considered a settlement, and they then would not be able to sue for additional damages if Bishop is subsequently found negligent. There are no solid decisions since it has only been days since the crisis. This sort of thing will most likely go on for years before liability is established, settlements with families are agreed to, and fines are levied by government agencies.

I have not seen any reference to LEAR_2008_17_Houston_Gas, and Wagner Jones is no longer the Vice President of EH&S.

There is a new fellow with that job, Sullivan Kimball. I have never met him, because I haven't done any work around the EH&S departments. I see an e-mail from Baldwin to Sullivan asking him to go through the files and check for anything that should be "sanitized." It is dated yesterday and so far there has been no reply.

The biggest trophy of the session is the conference call information contained in the meeting invitations on Baldwin's Outlook calendar. It has a dial-in number and participant code that allows someone on the other end of a telephone to participate in meetings. Such codes are issued to individuals, so all of Baldwin's teleconferences will have the same access information, including his weekly Monday calls with the executive team. It is so Bishop-like to use conference codes that don't change.

Companies that are more tech-savvy use WebEx meetings that have unique codes for each meeting and each participant, but once again, Bishop has elected the least costly alternative at the expense of security. With this information, I will be able to call in anonymously and listen each Monday to the confidential discussions among the highest rankers in the Bishop organization. I can also listen in on any other telephonic meetings that Baldwin originates. Now that I have access to his Outlook calendar, I know exactly when they are, whom they are with, and what they are about.

I'm not done, but my access time is just about up. I look at my watch and it is almost 10:00, and from the window by my terminal I can see my cab waiting across the street. I think about telling him to come back later and continuing my hacking, but I decide that might be rude to Beth. Besides, I am getting tired, and tomorrow will be a long day.

I leave the café, get in the cab, and thirty minutes later I'm pouring a glass of white wine from Beth's refrigerator. I am still out of cigarettes, but I know from previous visits that Beth keeps a carton in her pantry. I help myself and walk out to the patio for my evening tradition. It is dark but I can see Grant on the other side of the pool and walk over to him.

"Hi, Tanzie. We missed you at dinner. Where did you go?" Grant gets up and scoots one of the patio chairs closer to where he has been sitting.

"Nowhere, really," I lie. I sit down and take a sip of wine. "Took a cab and rode around for a while. Ended up going to Beck's for dinner."

"Wow. Better than ours, I'm sure." He laughs and leans toward me. "Sometimes I get so tired of this Paleo shit that Beth has me on."

"You two look fabulous, Grant. And what about Winston? Talk about a transformation," I say. "Who'da thunk it?"

"Yeah, he's shed a few pounds," Grant says, nodding.

I light my cigarette, take a long drag, and blow the smoke out of the corner of my mouth.

"Tanzie, did you hang on to any ownership interest in Winston's company?"

"No, I took the cash equivalent," I say, staring at the pool. "I thought about holding on to it but I really wanted to put as much distance between the two of us as possible. It was getting pretty ugly. Why?"

"That Bakken shale position has been going gangbusters," he says. "Word on the street is that he's selling out to one of the big players up there for a tidy sum."

"Why am I not surprised?" I groan. "His life is great and mine has gone to shit. He'll probably end up with some board seat and I'll be making Xerox copies of expense reports. Did you know he gave Rocky to Bill Matheson?"

"I hadn't heard that. But hang in there, Tanzie—things will get better."

"Thanks," I say. I hesitate. "I have an insurance question, Grant."

"Sure."

"Will Bishop's costs all be covered if it turns out they are responsible for the explosion?"

He looks at me. "That depends on a lot of things, like their coverage. Insurance can be complicated. I would imagine a company the size of Bishop has plenty of insurance, but everyone has a ceiling. If the costs exceed that ceiling, then they are on their own."

"Would there be any reason for the insurance not to pay?" I ask.

"Well, if the company didn't keep up their scheduled maintenance, perhaps. But that's fairly well controlled by the Department of Transportation. I'm not an expert, but I am pretty sure that Bishop would be required to file routinely with the agency and also have regular audits. Now of course if fraud is involved, that will be something else entirely. Why do you ask? Are you aware of something implicating them?"

"No," I react without thinking. "Actually, I'm not sure. I don't know what I think at this point, Grant. Those two boys. You saw them growing up. Every Fourth of July, every Easter egg hunt, every Halloween. I just find it horrible that their lives could be extinguished like that. And why? And who's to blame? Surely not the poor people who bought property not knowing they were sleeping over a powder keg. It's so unfair, Grant. It's unfair that our friends are gone."

"I agree one hundred percent, Tanzie. Did you happen to see Bill at the reception earlier? You know he's handling some of the suits."

"You told me that, but no, we didn't connect. I needed to get out of there."

"He was at dinner with us," Grant says. "I'm confident that Bill will get to the bottom of what happened and who's responsible. He's a bulldog; we all know that. I did mention that you worked for Bishop in the audit department. He seemed very interested in speaking with you."

I take a long last drag on my cigarette, put it out, and light another, trying to buy some time and figure out what to say. As angry as I am, I doubt I'm ready to hitch my wagon to Bill Matheson. Making Bill rich off information I discover doesn't sit well with me at the moment, even if it might help win a lawsuit. Plus, he has my dog.

"I'm just a flunky, Grant," I say finally. "I don't think I know anything relevant to the case."

"He's hosting a reception after the funeral tomorrow; maybe he can catch you there."

"Maybe. Thanks." I put out my fresh cigarette, watching it bend awkwardly in the ashtray. "I'll see you in the morning."

———◆———

I have trouble sleeping as I sort out all the information I discovered today. Did the LEAR really prove that Bishop was negligent? To me it does, but I am sure there are tons of legal and environmental loopholes that Bishop, with their infinite resources, can identify and exploit to their advantage. I don't know enough, and I am reluctant to disclose even to my closest friends what I have done, which I am quite sure is illegal.

I am up at six and make the coffee. It is raining, so I perch on a stool at the granite island watching the coffee drip. I have just poured a cup when Maria comes through the rear door, with a rain hat on her head and the *Chronicle* under her arm.

"Oh, Mrs. Lewis," she says, "you should have called me to make the coffee."

"No problem, Maria. I make my own every morning. I'm happy to do it."

"Can I make you some breakfast?"

"Toast, please," I answer.

"Oh, Mrs. Lewis, I am so sorry, but Mrs. McAfee, she does not like bread kept in the house."

"Eggs?"

"Whites, yes." With that, Maria gets busy pouring some clear stuff from a carton into a small bowl. I watch her add chopped vegetables, and by the time she puts it into the nonstick pan, it looks pretty appetizing. She cuts up some cantaloupe and opens a container of blueberries, and in minutes I have a low-carb, low-fat meal of the same type that keeps the McAfees, Mr. and Mrs., the envy of all those hoping to avoid the heartbreak of middle-age butt spread.

Beth comes down in her robe. Even with no makeup and her hair mussed, she looks great. If only Bishop subscribed to the meticulous preventive maintenance program used by Beth McAfee. It takes hard work and money to forestall old age, but clearly it is working in her case. She does not have that puffy look that so often results from too many procedures, and at sixty-two she looks much younger than I.

"I'll have the same, please," she tells Maria as she pours herself a cup of coffee and looks out the kitchen window. "Damn, it's raining."

"This is just the beginning," I say. I hand her the weather section of the paper that's calling for severe thunderstorms all day. Houston storms are legendary and can produce flash floods instantly due to low-pressure systems coming in off the Gulf. "I hope my flight home isn't delayed."

"I hope it is." Beth smiles. "I like having you here."

"I stole a pack of cigarettes from you last night," I confess. "Pressure, opportunity, and rationalization."

Beth laughs and she and I go out onto the covered porch for a smoke. I see Maria frown as she covers the skillet to keep Beth's eggs warm.

"So where did you end up going?" she asks as she positions her tiny behind into a swivel chair.

"Nowhere," I lie again. "Just drove around. How was dinner?"

"Strange. Very weird, coming from such a sad thing, that visitation. The whole family gone . . . just like that. No one wanted to talk about it, and it didn't seem appropriate to talk about anything else. Grant and I left pretty early; we were home by 9:00. Bill asked about you."

"So I heard," I say, swatting at a mosquito buzzing around my face. "I don't have anything that he'd be interested in."

"Maybe you can help him, you know, keep an ear to the ground and let him know what's going on from the inside."

"Well, unless he is curious about how invoices are coded, he's out of luck. I'm not very close to the action."

"Still, you never know." A clap of thunder that startles us interrupts the conversation. We extinguish our cigarettes and head back to the kitchen. "I'd better get dressed," I say, and leave Beth in the kitchen with Maria and her dried-out eggs.

———◆———

The funeral is at 9:30 at the St. John's Methodist church in River Oaks, not far from the McAfee home. On a nice day, we could have walked there, but given the weather, we have no choice but to drive.

As with the viewing at the funeral home, the church is packed, and we are grateful for the valet parking that allows us to avoid getting soaked. A funeral representative ushers us toward the front, handing Grant, one of the twenty-four pall-bearers required to manage the four caskets, a carnation to pin on his lapel. I see Winston and Caroline in a pew in front of us, noting that Winston, too, will be part of the casket crew. Grant leaves Beth and me and puts his hand on Winston's back, and the two of them head to the back of the church.

It is a sad service. Friends of Matt and Eric share stories of growing up together. Alice's sister Kate gives a wonderful trib-ute, and Ken's law partner gets everyone laughing about Ken's particular obsession with *Top Chef* and his numerous failed attempts to land a spot on the show. Ken had been quite sure that even as an amateur he could have wiped the floor with any chef in the country. The show's producers had sent him kind rejection letters, which Ken had then framed and hung in a guest bathroom off the garage.

I find myself crying through most of the service. Sadness about my friends gives way to thoughts about my own state of affairs. I know it is selfish to feel sorry for myself under the circumstances, but I just can't help it. Caroline and Winston will be in Scotland with the McAfees, and I won't. Not that I had expected Beth and Grant to cut off all ties with Winston or snub Caroline. I think they sort of hoped we could all become good friends and move past any hard feelings. Maybe if I remarry the right sort of man I can get right back in the circle. I know that's what Beth hopes. Lose some weight, get a facelift, take some Prozac, and get back out there. I don't blame my friends for thinking that way. In retrospect, I have been guilty of the same thing.

While I might do any one of those things, I am absolutely not interested in remarrying. I never again want to be dependent on a man for my sense of worth, even if it means giving up my friends. I will recapture my lost status on my own terms or not at all.

I realize that I have used the entire box of Kleenex that had been strategically placed in my pew. I shove the last one in my purse after composing myself as I file out of the church with my row.

The skies have cleared, but the dripping rainwater from the live oaks and building eaves sends the mourners into the parking lot for their after-service mingling while the valets scurry to retrieve all the cars.

I try to decide what to do now. The thought of being buttonholed by Bill Matheson at his house frightens me in my current state. I need more time to prepare before going head to head with that man. Besides, I'm not sure I can handle seeing good old Rocky and then having to leave him again.

I turn to Beth, who is fumbling with a tiny umbrella as she fishes through her purse in search of a cigarette.

"Want one?" she asks. "You can't smoke at Bill's. He's a fanatic after he quit last year. Had the whole place remodeled to remove all traces."

"Actually, no." I've been smoking way too much since being at Beth's. "Would you mind if I walk back to your house and then head to the airport? I'm afraid the traffic will be ridiculous with the weather."

Beth frowns as she lights up. "I guess not. We can give you a ride back to the house, though."

"That's okay, Beth. I could use the exercise."

"That's my girl." Beth smiles as she taps Grant, extricating him from an adjacent conversation circle. "Tanzie's decided to take off, Grant, better say good-bye."

Grant turns around and gives me a bear hug. "Don't be a stranger, Tanzie."

"I won't."

"Promise me you'll call or e-mail or just come down for a quick visit some weekend," Beth pleads. "Tulsa's not that far away."

"I promise," I lie, as I give Beth a good-bye hug.

As I walk away from the crowd and wait to cross the street, I realize that as much as I hate my life in Tulsa, Houston is not my home anymore. I find myself looking forward to the solitude of my little condo and the chance, though slight, of resurrecting my career all on my own.

return the rental car and ride the bus to terminal E at the airport. The flight board tells me my 1:30 Tulsa flight is delayed
until 4:30 due to weather. Many other flights are delayed as
well, and this, coupled with the crowds that typically travel on
Fridays, makes finding an available seat difficult. When Winston
and I traveled, we killed time at the Continental President's
Club since he had a membership as a company benefit. I am not
a member, and I knew I would not be allowed to enter without
being one. I had often witnessed weary travelers plead with the
front desk to let them in only to be pleasantly rejected and asked
to leave so that the legitimate members could be processed.

As I stand in front of the club entrance, I notice a man about
my age carrying a raincoat and briefcase heading through the
automatic doors to the President's Club. I take a chance and fol-

low right behind him into the entrance area. There is a line to get admitted.

"Awful weather," I say to him. "My flight is delayed for three hours."

"Mine too," he says.

We chat for a bit about things that strangers chat about in a line. The name on his briefcase tag is Jim Cleary, so when it is his turn to be processed, I tap him on the arm and say, loud enough for the attendant to hear, "Jim, I think they're ready for you." After he is validated I make eye contact with the gatekeeper, smile, and follow Jim in. As I'd planned, the attendant assumes I am Jim's better half. Jim doesn't even notice me behind him as he gets on the escalator and heads up to the bar. I separate from my imaginary husband, make myself a cup of tea, and find a cozy spot by a window with a view of the flight schedule.

"Mind if I sit here?" asks a gray-haired, bulldog-faced stranger.

"No, not at all." I gesture to the tufted leather chair across from a cocktail table that defines my ill-gotten territory.

"Buster Connelly, N'awlins, Louisiana." He extends his hand to shake mine.

"Tanzie Lewis."

Back in my career days, when I flew nonstop, I would avoid this kind of situation by placing a *Watchtower* booklet on my lap after my seat belt had been securely fastened. Then, even if people had to sit next to me, they usually avoided eye contact and kept their nose in a book. Once a real Jehovah's Witness sat down next to me, but since my *Watchtower* indicated that I had already been saved and needed no evangelizing, there was no need for much discussion, so I quietly dozed undisturbed until landing.

Now, with Buster, I try to signal that I am not interested in making a long-lasting relationship by looking back down at my book. But he is not to be deterred, and thus begins one of those one-sided conversations that are impossible to get out of. I peer around, but there are no other seats and plenty of folks are standing around waiting to lunge at the next vacancy, even if it involves being stuck in a conversational bear trap. I can leave and stand for three hours, or I can make polite conversation with Buster from NOLA.

"Where you off to on this rainy day?" he asks, stirring something brown over ice with his index finger. Buster's face has that red tinge and bulbous nose that comes from steady consumption of such brown liquids over many years.

"Tulsa." I give an impersonal smile then look back down at my book.

"Oh my, my, Tulsa—just love that town. Tell me, Tanzie from Tulsa—you are from Tulsa, right? That's just too cute—Tanzie from Tulsa." He laughs at his joke and doesn't wait for a response. "Tell me, Tanzie from Tulsa, what do you do? Are you here on bidness?"

"I'm an accountant, but I'm in Houston for personal reasons."

"Oh, a bean counter! Don't know how you can do all that tedious bookkeeping. Me, I couldn't stand those classes. Put me to sleep. Takes all kinds, though, I guess. I'm the owner of Tiger Offshore Petroleum in N'awlins. I'm down here visiting some bankers."

I could ask him if he knows Winston or tell him I work for Bishop, but I am not in the mood for talking—an arrangement that works very well for Buster. By the end of my three-hour sentence I have learned that Buster graduated from LSU in 1977, pledged Sigma Nu fraternity, started out with Gulf, worked in consulting, and then ventured out on his own. He is married, with a grown son in California and a daughter in Dallas. He has five grandchildren who are all exceptional in every damned endeavor out there. He shows me pictures of them from an overstuffed wallet and drones on and on about every utterance any of them have ever mouthed. Buster has season tickets to the Saints, Hornets, and LSU home games. He usually travels by Netjet, but his secretary screwed up his travel arrangements (excuse his French).

"What do you think about the explosion?" I ask when Buster finally comes up for air.

"Well, now, seems everyone wants cheap gas in their car but they don't want a pipeline under their house. Pipeline explosions are rare things, you know. Tragic? Yes they are. Do we try to prevent them? Yes we do. But in the end, it's just a cost of doing bidness. There is no other way to transport product economically."

Here's another person equating lost lives to operating expenses. I am emotionally spent and all out of fight, so I let his insensitive remarks go unchallenged.

"Do you want a pipeline under yours?" I finally ask him.

He ignores that. "Pipelines are the safest method of transportation for petroleum products," Buster begins, and he goes on from there for an eternity. I have heard this speech before from the Bishop brothers and from Winston before them. *Fine,* I think, *but they still need to be maintained to be safe. Cutting corners to save money is like stealing from everyone else.*

At last my watch tells me I can leave. "Well, Buster, my flight is boarding," I say, getting up and starting to gather my carry-ons.

"Maybe we'll run into each other again." Buster stands up, demonstrating that he has been properly schooled in Southern manners. "Here's my card, Tanzie from Tulsa. If you're ever in the Big Easy, gimme a call. We can continue our conversation."

"Thank you, Buster. Safe travels." As I head to the escalator, I notice an abandoned *Handelsblatt*, the German financial newspaper. I fold it and stick it into the exterior pocket of my bag. Not as good as a *Watchtower*, but an adequate prop for my "Ich spreche kein Englisch" response should anyone try to strike up a conversation with me on the flight home.

———◆———

I return to the Bishop building at 8:00 a.m. on Saturday to do the busywork Frank has given me. Once again, there is no security manning the desk, so I badge in and head for the elevator bank servicing the sixth floor. I log in and complete Frank's request in less than an hour.

Frank is a guy who overcomplicates things, so for him even the most inconsequential task takes hours to think through, evaluate in every detail, and then execute and re-execute as new issues pop into his pea brain. I am usually able to isolate the core objective, make a decision, and then produce a workable result quickly and efficiently. Though not specifically identified by Dante, there is indeed a ring of hell where punishment involves being an underling to an idiot boss. I have no idea what I have done to deserve this punishment but I have lots of company, particularly at Bishop.

I hit *send* so Frank will have my work and also see that I produced it over the weekend. I am about to leave, but being alone in the office gets my curiosity juices flowing. Remembering Moe's request to continue with the building security review, I decide to go exploring. Snooping is exciting for me, and I enjoy having access to every part of the operation. If I go too far, well, I am just a go-getter who got carried away, not a criminal.

It isn't as if they will even notice if I steal anything—say, a million dollars. I think about this idea for a while. The controls are so bad at Bishop that I am convinced that I could figure out a way to steal a million if I were so inclined. Maybe every board should ask Internal Audit to attempt to steal that amount just to test how secure their company really is. Trouble is, what if the internal auditor decides not to give the money back? Living on the run or in exile seems like a tall order for a few million, no matter how great John Grisham makes it look.

I wander up to the ninth floor and enter the cube farm near the western corner of the building, where Mazie's desk is. I sit in her black cloth chair and wonder what it feels like to be her. How does it feel to work every day with the same people you are secretly stealing from? How does it feel to make chitchat at the coffee bar, talking about a TV show or your grandkids or the winning pass by the college quarterback, all the things that make office acquaintances think they know you? What would Elly May Clampett think?

I recall Bennet Bishop referring to us employees as "family" during one of the quarterly all-employee meetings. "We are the Bishop family," he said. *Bullshit*, I think. *We are certainly not family. You don't pay family to show up every day.* Further, if I truly were related to Bennet, I would be back on the golf course rather than producing meaningless work for the numbskulls on the sixth floor. No, I am not a member of the family; I suppose Mazie isn't either.

I start rummaging around inside her desk. Mazie doesn't keep her password in the usual places, but she does not lock her desk either. I go through her desk drawers one by one and come up empty. I notice a two-drawer file cabinet under her desk that is locked, and I am unable to find the key anywhere. I help myself to candy left in a bowl in a neighbor's cube and stuff the wrappers into my back pocket so as not to create a trash trail exposing my unauthorized access to the Accounts Payable department. But search as I may, I cannot find Mazie's password or any other personal details other than a couple of framed pictures of the grandkids. Leave it to the thief to take security seriously.

I continue my search in the Accounts Payable area, scoring big time at the candy lady's cube. I suppose she thought it was clever to embed her password in a grocery list kept in a manila folder by her desk. But I knew that trick and noticed 6#sParsley immediately. Who would ever buy six pounds of parsley, anyway? I did give her partial credit; this was not the same as leaving it under a pen set. I hit a couple more floors on the lower levels, and by noon I have sixteen passwords, a list of Social Security numbers I discovered in an HR wastebasket, and a copy of a potential acquisition memo found at a printer in one of the Environmental Health and Safety work areas. I feel bored and decide I have enough information for one day; it is all too easy.

As I exit the elevator, I notice the janitorial crew heading to the executive elevator bank, which I had used to ride up to the thirtieth floor almost a week ago with Keith. On impulse and with total disregard for Moe's instructions, I step in behind them as they get on the elevator, exit with them on the twenty-fifth floor, and piggyback in as they open the secure door that leads to Business Development and Treasury. This is an unexpected triumph. I smile at the cleaning women who assume I belong on the floor. I pass them and head for an empty office to figure out what to do next. Spanish chitchat is drowned out by the hum of vacuums as the women go about their work. Saturdays are the deep clean days, which means offices are unlocked to perform the extra duties. I decide to walk the floor and snoop around; a password here could prove useful. Not for Moe's audit, but for my own surveillance of Bishop activities.

I stop by the coffee bar adjacent to a locked wing, and to my astonishment, I see a keychain hanging out of the lock of a door propped open with a trash can. This is the mother lode. There are not only keys on the chain but also security cards for the entire building. As I take the keys and head back to the elevators, I feel a little guilty about the theft. Surely one of the cleaners will lose her job over this. I wonder, too, if the theft will result in security changing locks and badge configurations. I will just have to wait and see. Most likely, I figure, the janitorial group for this building will not report the loss and instead just work around with their additional sets of keys rather than risk all of them getting dumped.

Now, I can easily use the key cards to get up to the thirtieth floor and poke around, but I decide to get out of the building and save any additional recon for another day. I need time to figure out what to do with all this new access. I try to keep calm as I settle into my car but cannot help feeling the nervous excitement of having done something dangerous.

I decide to continue snooping in Baldwin's computer. Tulsa does not have an Internet café, so I head to the public library near downtown.

"Excuse me," I ask the librarian at the desk by the entrance. "Do you have Internet terminals for the public?"

"Why yes we do, ma'am. Right over there." She points to a row of computer stations between the fiction and the children's section.

I grab a terminal near the back and scoot the thinly padded chair underneath me. After hitting Bishop's remote system, I log in as Baldwin and access the webmail on the monitor screen. I notice instantly that many of the e-mails I had read Thursday have now been deleted. I read what's there, but nothing too juicy remains in the account. I suppose Baldwin is being careful. I check his calendar and notice that he is in meetings with the insurance folks, lawyers, and the executive team for the next two weeks almost straight.

I log in as Marla, and she too has purged any explosion-related correspondence on which she had been copied. All that remains are the e-mails organizing lunches, business trips, and other benign communications. I access Marla's LEAR file, but LEAR_2008_17_Houston_Gas is gone. To me this is a clear signal that Bishop is trying to eliminate any evidence that they knew or should have known that the Houston pipeline was corroded.

So far, I haven't run across any evidence that corrosion is in fact the cause; it could have been a construction crew or terrorism. Still, it turns my stomach to think they are preparing to dodge responsibility for their decision not to take preventive measures in 2008. As far as I know, I have the only copy of LEAR_2008_17_Houston _Gas in existence, and now I have a responsibility to manage that information, even if I have obtained it illegally.

I feel a sense of importance for the first time in years, but at the same time I am terrified at the thought of mishandling it. This is not a Monday morning staff meeting, after all. I think about calling Bill Matheson to get some advice, but that doesn't appeal to me; some big ego directing every move and cutting me out of decisions. I shake off my momentary lapse in confidence as I pull the flash drive and zip it into a secure compartment inside my purse. This is going to be great. If nothing else, it is an adventure of a lifetime.

"Did you find what you needed?" asks the librarian as I walk toward the glass doors leading to the parking lot.

"And then some." I smile back at her as I make my exit.

CHAPTER TEN

The Sunday morning call from Lucy rings right on schedule, and I am in a heavy terry bathrobe sipping coffee on my balcony. Our conversation turns immediately to the explosion and how Lucy has known all along that "those people" I'm working for are evil.

"I'm beginning to agree with you," I tell her, and I explain that my friends were casualties and what I have found in the files so far.

"What else do you have?" she asks after I tell her about reviewing the LEAR folders.

"I don't know. I haven't been through everything yet. This has all been really fast."

"Why don't you send me what you have and I'll take a look?" Lucy offers.

I hesitate. "I don't think it's a good idea to send the files over the Internet, Lucy. I'm trying to be very careful. Taking those files was illegal, and I really don't want to take a chance, even a remote chance, that anything gets traced back to me."

What I don't tell her is that I know my sister better than myself. She is an environmental fanatic who is likely to include kindred spirits on our communication if she isn't under careful supervision. While I'm fairly sure that Lucy would not do anything without my consent, I am not comfortable sending incriminating files to someone who thinks jail time is a badge of honor when it's for holding up environmental principles. The temptation might be too much for her.

Still, Lucy is brilliant. As Uncle Agamemnon summed up one day, "Tanzie smart, Lucy smarter." A painful but true assessment, I have to admit. She has an undergraduate degree in chemical engineering from Cal Tech and a master's degree in environmental sciences from Stanford. In her younger days, before venturing out into the world of colored cotton and sheep, Lucy worked in the oilfields wearing a hazmat suit that now doubles as her beekeeping outfit. She would no doubt be an excellent source of help in figuring out what other mayhem besides blowing up sleeping Houstonians the Bishop boys are covering up.

"How about coming to Tulsa, Lucy? We can work on this together. I haven't seen you in ages."

"I told you before, I have sheep issues," she starts, but she almost immediately reverses course. "But I'll make it work, somehow. I can only stay for a couple of days, though. Can you pay for the flight, Tanzie? I have zero cash at the moment."

Her sudden enthusiasm to leave her beloved farm gives me pause. It is common knowledge in our family that Lucy rarely travels anymore. In her middle age she has become neurotic about food and prefers to control every bit of what she eats by growing it herself. She is hugely suspicious of mass-produced food and convinced that the genetically modified varieties are the reason for the obesity and bad health of most Americans. On her farm she grows or raises just about every morsel she eats. She even grows her own wheat for flour and churns her own butter. I sometimes refer to her as the original little red hen.

The lure of getting involved in something that could potentially harm those evil Bishop boys must be compelling.

"Now look, Lucy," I warn. "I want to be very clear before I formally include you in this. You absolutely cannot breathe a word about this to anyone. You cannot send files anywhere without asking me first. If you don't think you can follow my rules before you commit to helping me, you need to let me know right now."

There is a pause on the line, and I can tell Lucy is offended by my preemptive accusation. I suppress the urge to offer a quick apology and wait.

"Got it." Again, there is some dead air.

"Hey, I'm sorry, Lucy. I'm just so terrified about all of this. On the one hand, this is so exciting and the first interesting thing I've done in years. But on the other hand, I'm worried that I'll make some mistake and wind up in jail or in the papers."

"Or perhaps let evil fiends get away with murder," Lucy suggests.

"Yes, that too," I say. "And yes, I get it. It's not all about me."

"I know you do." That is a lie. Lucy has always considered me a selfish sort. She really wants in, though, I can tell. "It'll be thrilling, Tanzie," she says. "We'll make a good team. I promise I won't go all WikiLeaks on you."

"You realize the last time we worked together, you wound up in bankruptcy court. Are you sure you want to become involved?" I ask, getting another painful subject out of the way.

"That wasn't you; that was Winston," she says happily. "I'll get online and send you some flight times that work for me. I can't wait to see you, Tanzie."

"Me too. Love you, Lucy!" I hang up, grinning genuinely for the first time in quite a while. I already feel much more comfortable having someone smart to bounce information off of. Lucy is right. This is going to be fun. Shadowy, dangerous fun.

———◆———

As I stand under the hot shower, it occurs to me that I should probably go over to the office and snoop around some more. Thanks to the cleaning crew, I now have access to every floor and restricted area at Bishop. Given the explosion and all the extra work going on, I am fairly sure that the building will not be abandoned like it was last week at Easter, but most weekend workers probably won't be there until after church. I can always say I am doing an audit, even if I'm not. Hal might get mad, but so what. I can defray any bad PR with the fraud I have discovered. That would be fairly good insurance against being fired for putting my nose where it didn't belong.

I dry my hair, get dressed, and head over to the Bishop building. As I cross the street, I am surprised to see two women leaving the building through the huge glass doors on the north side. It is Mazie and a friend who looks familiar. While Mazie is clearly in her fifties, the other woman is probably mid-thirties and quite attractive. "Hi there, Mazie," I say cheerfully. Mazie seems nervous but smiles. I wonder for a minute if she is on to me. "I thought I was the only one who had to work weekends around here."

They both smile, but neither seems to want to make small talk.

"Bless your heart," Mazie says finally as she moves past me. "Don't work too hard!"

Mazie's behavior piques my interest. It is fairly common for fraudsters to work after hours and on weekends. Maybe I can find something incriminating in her desk this time. So, instead of getting off on six, I decide to get off on nine and walk directly to Mazie's cube. I cannot believe my luck when instead of a blank screen or the three grandchildren, I see the blue Windows screen staring back at me. Computers left unattended usually revert to a screen saver after about five or ten minutes of inactivity and require an ID and password to log back in. It is best to manually log out every time you leave your computer, but hardly anyone ever does.

Maybe Mazie and her friend have only gone to get something to eat and will be returning. I will have to keep my ears open. Most likely she and her buddy are off to worship with Elly May. I access the settings screen and disable the automatic log off feature. That way I am free to do some exploring without worrying that I'll be kicked out in the middle of accessing Mazie's files.

I leave Mazie's cube, looking for another monitor that is still logged on. I go up and down the row of cubes but find nothing. I decide to check the offices and still come up empty. I make a quick stop at the candy lady's cube to score a mini Kit Kat or two. As I shove the chocolate into my mouth and the wrapper into my pocket, my eyes are drawn to a family photo that's tacked to the canvas bulletin board under some hanging cabinets. The picture is a mom, dad, three preschool-aged girls, and an overweight black doggie with white around its muzzle.

The woman is Mazie's friend—a little younger, perhaps, but I am sure that's who it is. Amy Larson, I read off the nameplate hanging from her cube's exterior wall. During my time in Mazie's cube, Amy's computer has reverted to the login screen, but I found her password yesterday during my security sweep, so if I want to, I can get in. I wonder what kind of car she drives; if she and Mazie are in cahoots, probably a Mercedes minivan with all those kids.

I return to Mazie's cube and access her Outlook account to read her e-mail. Nothing exciting here: just some approvals for vendor setup, Bishop communications, and daily Pottery Barn sales alerts. The woman with her had me contemplating whether there is more to her scheme than I have found so far. I wonder if she might be an accomplice. The vendor fraud I found while doing Frank's test was strictly a one-person gig. When two or more people are involved in a fraud, it's referred to as collusion. With collusion, controls that rely on segregation of duties for their effectiveness are compromised. Fraudsters tend to work alone.

As Ben Franklin said, "Three may keep a secret, as long as two of them are dead." Involving more than one person in a crime increases risk exponentially, and you can never fully trust someone else not to turn you in if it saves his or her hide. But if Mazie does have an accomplice, she can get away with a much bigger take, potentially in the millions. I now feel curious to test out some fairly typical scenarios. The first step is to find out exactly what her access allows her to do. I bring up the invoice-processing screen of her accounting software. All the fields are grayed out, which means Mazie cannot process a voucher for payment. Pretty typical.

I go to the vendor maintenance screen and am trying to figure out how to set up a vendor when I hear the elevator ding and two female voices getting progressively louder.

"Shit," I whisper and freeze momentarily to assess my limited options.

Staying cool under pressure is one of my best traits. It has allowed me to sink long putts when needed to clinch many a championship in my day. Thinking swiftly, I decide it is better to at least try to make a hasty exit, and I hit the Windows icon, click on the shutdown tab, and click on *log off*. I don't have enough time to get to the stairs or elevator without being seen, so I grab my purse, crawl into an empty office, and hide under the desk. My activity makes the automatic overhead office light turn on. I suppress panic, tell myself to stay calm, and take a deep breath.

"Is Jane here?" I hear Mazie ask as they walk by.

"I didn't see her earlier," Amy replies. From the volume of their voices, I can tell they are standing in the office doorway. Beads of sweat are forming on my brow from a stress-induced hot flash. It is a very real possibility that they might walk around Jane's desk and find me.

"Go check the coffee bar," Mazie barks as she approaches the desk.

I hold my breath, trying to think of an excuse. Hide and seek? Testing evasive tactics if a crazed gunman comes in and shoots up the place? I close my eyes.

I remain absolutely still even when I hear Mazie's foot bump the bottom of Jane's desk. Has she seen me? I hear Mazie leave Jane's office.

"No one's in the coffee bar," I hear Amy report.

"Her computer's not on and I didn't see a purse. Must have been a janitor or someone from financial reporting stopping by. I think we're okay."

The sound of footsteps gets fainter as they head toward the cubes down the hallway.

"Stupid janitor's been eating my candy," Amy complains casually.

I can hear their conversation, which means they will hear me if I make any noise.

I am dying to get out of the tight space and rub my calf that has started to cramp. The waiting is almost unbearable. I long to stretch but don't dare.

To pass the time I go over in my head what they might be up to—Mazie setting up fictitious vendors and Amy processing them through, perhaps. There might be some additional steps required, but that's generally how a two-crook operation in accounts payable works. A loud ping from my purse gives me a fright. Once again I freeze, but it doesn't seem as if they heard anything.

"Almost done, Mom?" I hear Amy ask. "I need a smoke break."

Mom! This is making sense now.

"Give me five minutes and then we can go," I hear Mazie say.

"Okay, I'll meet you outside."

The best accomplices are family. Just ask the O'Leary girls. I smile as I recall an incident from my teenage days in San Francisco.

When Lucy and I were in high school, we both had after-school jobs at Joseph Magnin, a high-end department store in downtown San Francisco. Lucy was sixteen and worked in the gift-wrapping station. I had lied about my age and at fifteen was hired in the Juniors department.

When it came time for our eighteen-year-old sister, Blondie, to graduate, our mother and Mrs. Cosmos, across the street, had fixed Blondie up with Spiro Cosmos to go to their high school prom together. Neither Blondie nor Spiro was very excited about the other, but since neither had any better option, both agreed to go along with the arrangement.

"Blondie, that dress is way too small," I said as she handed me the silver lamé gown to ring up one afternoon in late April. Chubby Blondie was always on a diet, but discipline was not her long suit, so the regimens never lasted more than a day or two.

"I'll go on a diet. I have a month before the dance. It'll be good incentive for me."

I shook my head. There was no way Blondie, at least a fourteen, was going to skinny down to a size eight in a month, but I knew better than to take issue with her delusion. The dress cost more than $100, a huge sum in those days, and it represented at least a month's worth of tips from her waitress job.

At home, Blondie hung the dress on the closet door so she could look at it every morning when she got up, presumably to keep the lasagna at bay. Still, as the days wore on, it was clear that her goal was unrealistic, and panic was starting to percolate inside her.

The hair salon at Magnin's was at the top of a curved ornate staircase with red plush carpet that was the focal point of the store entrance. The Juniors department was right next to the salon, and I waved to Blondie when she came in for her hair appointment the Saturday of the dance.

"What are you going to do, Blondie? Can we find you another dress?"

"I have a plan. But keep quiet. No matter what. Okay?"

"Okay," I said and went back to my department.

A few minutes later I heard a scream from near the staircase and watched as customers and employees ran over to see what had happened. There at the foot of the staircase was Blondie, legs akimbo. Even from the top of the stairs I could tell she wasn't hurt badly, so I ran and got Lucy.

We charged down the stairs and told the store manager, Mr. Gamble, that this was our sister.

"We've called an ambulance. It should be here shortly. We are so sorry this happened."

"Lipstick," Blondie mumbled. "Lipstick."

Lucy and I exchanged looks. I went to the top of the staircase and there on the second step was a Revlon lipstick in Passionate Pink. It looked brand new.

"Is this yours?" I asked Blondie as the paramedics were loading her onto a stretcher.

"No. That's not my shade," Blondie answered

dramatically. "I think I sprained my ankle. Does it look swollen?"

Lucy and I looked at Blondie's ankles. Each looked as chubby as the other.

"Hard to tell," Lucy replied.

Mr. Gamble let us both off work to accompany Blondie to the hospital, where the doctor wrapped one of her ankles in an ace bandage. Not a serious injury, he told us, but she should stay off of it for a few days just to be safe. A nurse came by with some crutches for her to use.

"If you didn't want to go to the prom, Blondie, why didn't you just pretend to be sick? That's what anyone else would have done," I said while we waited for the number 2 Clement Muni bus to take us home.

"No one would have believed me," Blondie said. "They would have thought I was faking."

Mama just sighed and muttered some Greek expression under her breath when the three of us arrived at the house. She was well acquainted with how Blondie's mind worked and must have suspected the injury was neither real nor accidental. Still, she didn't pursue the matter beyond what we told her. Spiro sent flowers and candy to the house and we spent the evening watching the *Mary Tyler Moore Show* and eating chocolates. In an effort to thwart a lawsuit, Mr. Gamble refunded the cost of Blondie's gown, which Lucy wore to her prom two years later.

Blondie never worried that Lucy or I would tell Mama or Mr. Gamble about her caper. She understood the bond between sisters too well. The following week when I found a Rexall Drug receipt for one Passionate Pink lipstick in the wastebasket I was emptying, I tore it into tiny pieces.

Fifteen minutes later I hear the joyful sound of Mazie packing up. With the ding of the elevator signaling her departure, I emerge from my hiding place, stiff and aching.

I skedaddle back to my cube on the sixth floor, lest Mazie or Amy forget something and return. I pop a couple of Advil, washing them down with the glass of water on my desk that I abandoned on Saturday. I fish through my purse to read the text whose ding was almost my undoing. It is from Lucy. *Call me. Flights are expensive.*

This can wait, I decide, and I quickly log in to my computer and access the testing I worked on last week. I pull the payment file and this time filter for vendors set up by Mazie and processed by Amy. Mazie can't process an invoice on her own, but with her daughter able to, the control structure has been breached. There are too many to see any pattern, so I review the payment instructions looking for red flags such as PO boxes or foreign wire accounts. The list is much smaller now, and I can see, as I suspected, that this fraud is much bigger than what I had previously found.

In addition to the changing of a legitimate vendor's banking information back and forth, there are at least five fictitious vendors—among them Larson Consulting, MCAL Electric, and other parts of their names or initials—whose checks are sent to PO boxes, and others are sent to what appear to me to be Cayman accounts. I know what Cayman accounts look like because

Winston and I used to have a place on Seven Mile Beach for years and wired the annual maintenance fee. When the condo sold, I kept my half in a Cayman account so as not to repatriate my funds and avoid—or better, "defer"—U.S. taxes.

Bishop has international operations, and foreign payments are not unusual, so it is unlikely that anyone who isn't already suspicious will notice the foreign activity. It looks to me like the PO box scheme started two years ago, while the Cayman wires to three similar vendors began fairly recently. It is typical of fraudsters to start slowly and then build up their operation as they gain a better understanding of the system and what gets caught and—most important—what does not. My initial calculations put the theft well into the millions of dollars, and it seems to have increased dramatically in recent months.

This is huge. Bigger than Moe's South Texas fraud. It is the type of thing that auditors learn about but rarely see firsthand. More common are forged expense report receipts or stolen inventory, little stuff by comparison. This really could be a promotion for me. Regardless of how evil the Bishops are, a change in title from Staff Auditor to Principal or Consultant would do wonders for my résumé. I might even be invited to speak at a conference or audit roundtable.

I decide not to go back to the ninth floor since I wasted so much time hiding under Jane's desk. I want to hack into Baldwin's e-mail, and I want to make sure it cannot be traced to my computer if someone looks into it later.

I grab a lunch at Braum's, a favorite Oklahoma creamery, on my way out of downtown. No wonder I am gaining weight. Mason is right: What do I expect with a diet of candy and milkshakes? Heading south to the same library I used the day before, I marvel at the true beauty of Tulsa's early spring. After the coldest damn winter I have ever experienced, spring has come. As if overnight, the town has been painted in white blossoms from the Bradford pears and then bright pink with redbuds. Tulips have sprung up and pansies, sparse and leggy during the winter, have erupted to blanket the landscape in deep purple and yellow.

Southeast Texas is completely different. Houston is tropical, which means there are really only two seasons: hot as hell and beautiful. Occasionally a cold front will blow in, and it may get to as low as the teens, but only for a single day, and then it goes back to the high fifties or mid-sixties. Generally, you cannot tell the season there by the landscape.

My phone rings. I don't like to talk on the phone while driving, but I remember Lucy's text and don't want her to have to wait.

"Why didn't you call me, Tanzie?" she chides.

"God, I'm sorry. It's been a busy morning."

"I found a flight, but it's $1,500 round trip. I didn't want to make the reservation without getting your okay first."

"Fine. What time do you get in?"

"Not until 10:30 at night. There's a three-hour layover in Houston."

One problem with Tulsa is that it is very difficult to travel into and out of. There are only direct flights to a handful of hubs. All other destinations require connections, which add time and potential delays and lost luggage. I used to laugh at an upscale seafood restaurant that bragged that their fish was flown in daily. If it takes me twelve hours to get to the coast, what chance does a fish have? I pull over and give Lucy my credit card information, and she gives me the flight numbers.

"Thanks, Tanzie. See you tomorrow. This is going to be great!"

"If it's as much fun as hiding from two accounts payable clerks all morning, I'm not so sure."

"What are you talking about?"

"Nothing. I'll tell you later."

The library is empty, and I resume my spot at the back computer. As anxious as I am to hack into Baldwin's computer, I am fixated on knowing exactly how the Mazie/Amy caper is carried out. I'm still not sure how Amy can process the invoices without a third person providing electronic approval. I log in as Amy Larson and goof around on her accounting software. Amy cannot set up a vendor, but she can enter an invoice that then has to be approved by someone else. I knew from my previous audits that each invoice has to be entered by one clerk and approved by another.

Most companies have the engineer or manager who authorized the work perform the electronic approval. Bishop, however, is woefully behind the times and has clung to paper copies of things long after others, including their software manufacturer, have moved to paperless systems. So at Bishop, the approving manager submits a paper invoice to Accounts Payable, where Amy or an equivalent clerk enters it into the system as pending. Then it's approved electronically by the other accounts payable clerk, who relies on a signature on the paper copy. After that electronic approval is entered, the payment will process, and checks are cut or wires are sent without additional human interaction.

The process is excruciatingly inefficient, and vendors complain often and loudly about how long it takes for them to get paid. Still, Bishop is big and a good client for most, so the extra time required for payment is just a cost of doing business.

I wonder if there is a third person involved in the scheme. It is large enough to satisfy the criminal greed of an entire ring. Someone other than Amy has to be approving the invoices; the system requires it, and it cannot be Mazie. I need to do a little more research before presenting this to Frank, but that can wait until tomorrow morning. Then, I can look at the payments to see if there is a common approver, which might imply another ring member or two.

I log in as Baldwin, noting right away an e-mail from Sullivan Kimball to Bishop explaining the results of his research. The memo references LEAR_2008_17_Houston_Gas and indicates that back then Wagner Jones had put together a task force to determine how best to assess the condition of the Galleria section of pipe. The most expensive alternative required remapping the pipeline to determine exactly where it was, as well as gaining access to certain of the properties in order to perform excavation.

Wagner's team had been in contact with the property division, but no one had been able to find the right-of-way records. Each parcel had potentially needed to be renegotiated with the current owner to gain access, and that had the potential to add time and money to the project. Furthermore, if corrosion were found, they would have had to shut down the pipeline for several months to make necessary replacements, adding loss of revenue to the ever-depleting bottom line.

A cheaper alternative was mentioned involving a "smart pig" that might have been able to adjust for the difference in pipe diameter. Wagner had been getting bids from some companies in Houston, but Sullivan couldn't find any of those proposals in the files. As far as Sullivan could tell, the Houston project got tabled when a crude leak in Kansas consumed the limited EH&S resources, and Wagner was diagnosed with lung cancer and retired in January 2009. Apparently the Houston project had fallen through the cracks when Sullivan took over the department.

Baldwin had responded with an e-mail asking for an in-person meeting to discuss this further. Instead of "Sincerely" or "Kind Regards," Baldwin had concluded his email "Chapped."

I download the e-mail to my flash drive, lest Baldwin decide to erase this correspondence as he had the others.

Just as I am about log off, the computer screen goes to the home page. *Press Control+Alt+Delete* is on the screen. Then it flashes: *This computer is locked and being used by another user BRBishop.*

I jump back. "Shit!" I look up but no one is around me to complain.

I'm not sure what just happened. Could the message mean that Baldwin logged on and the computer kicked me off? Could he figure out that I was in his computer remotely? My palms begin to sweat and a hot flash erupts in my cheeks. I gather my things and hurry out of the library.

Once home, glass of wine and cigarette in hand, I feel a bit calmer. He probably didn't even notice. I noticed because I got kicked off. I decide it will be best to pose a hypothetical question along those lines to Todd and find out what went on at Baldwin's end of the screen, and not to expend energy worrying about the unknown. Instead, I focus on other details.

Baldwin and Bennet's meeting with Sullivan tomorrow evening will be important, and I am annoyed that it will take place face to face. Maybe there will be a write-up recapping the discussion in someone's email, but that might be a stretch. On the surface, the pipeline issue is plain enough. One crisis is replaced by a bigger one and then gets forgotten altogether. Still, I desperately want to better understand the Bishop Group's "going forward strategy" in all of this. Surely it will not be confined to deleting files and keeping their fingers crossed. Maybe something will be discussed in the Monday executive session I plan to call into. I will just have to wait and see.

CHAPTER ELEVEN

The Monday morning executive meeting is scheduled for 8:00 a.m., an hour and a half before our weekly Internal Audit update in Hal's office. I dial the conference number at five minutes till from my cube, using an earbud to ensure my privacy. If someone walks by, that person will think I am listening to music while I work. After yesterday, I am committed to planning everything I do and figuring out plausible explanations for my behavior just in case. I don't want to find myself crammed under another desk any time soon.

"Welcome to the one-source Instameet conferencing center," says a pleasant female computer voice. "Please enter your passcode followed by the pound or hash key."

I enter my code.

"You are the fifth person to join the conference. At the tone, please say your name and then press the pound symbol."

The tone sounds, and I press pound without identifying myself. I have witnessed Hal and others making conference calls, and they never identify themselves. I wait for someone to ask who has just joined, but no one does.

I can hear talking among the conference room attendees, but the meeting has not officially started yet.

"Let's begin, gentlemen," Baldwin says at exactly eight o'clock.

Each business unit head takes a turn at articulating the anticipated weekly events from deals in the works, progress on large projects, or market conditions that could impact expected financial results. It is no surprise to me that the European operations are suffering big time due to their recession. Things are not great in most of the domestic units either, but none of that is as bad as the looming problem of the Texas situation.

"As you are aware, I have been in contact with our EH&S group to help us understand the events leading up to the Houston pipeline explosion," says someone. "We will be having a special meeting this evening with legal and EH&S to better understand our options going forward on this."

"Skip, are you on the line?" This sounds like Bennet. Skip is the vice president in charge of Human Resources, who from all appearances is not part of the normal meeting guest list. He is calling in from his office on twenty-nine rather than joining the celebrities on thirty.

"Yes, sir."

"Perhaps you can update the group here on Project Titanic."

"Sure, Bennet. My team is exploring opportunities to rebalance our general administrative costs given the expected increase in legal fees and potential settlements and fines should

Bishop be held liable for the Houston situation. We are currently exploring many strategic alternatives, such as outsourcing certain corporate functions or evaluating other departments as fit for purpose. As you may remember, we had started a similar initiative three months ago when the crude markets became 'backwardated' and the marine segment encountered some headwinds, so much of the legal legwork has been easy to leverage. Our timeline on this is to begin this morning with some top-level items and have something to you gentlemen by next Monday's meeting on the broader elements. This is aggressive, of course, but we are committed to adding value during this critical time at Bishop."

HR tends to speak its own language, but my rough interpretation is that cost cuts will have to be made so that Bishop's bottom line can absorb the costs of killing my friends and their neighbors. Instead of the top executives taking the hit in their salaries or annual bonuses, the pain will be shifted to the rank-and-file employees, who will find themselves out of work in one of the worst recessions since the Great Depression. It seems that some of the firings will occur today, since it sounds to me as though they went down this path pretty recently but abandoned it for unknown reasons. HR, of course, is hoping to be spared from the cutbacks by proving that they are great team players. Good luck with that.

In layoffs, generally the higher-ups don't get fired the same day as everyone else. Top brass brings them in separately to discuss their enormous contribution to the company that will no longer be needed, assure them that they will find something great in no time, and inform them that if they do not sign the severance agreement or if they hire a lawyer they'll forgo their "package." Some of these packages can be quite lucrative: a year or two of pay, full bonus, vested stock options, and covered medical plans.

I suddenly wonder if I will be part of the layoff, and I am horrified. I was lucky to get this job, and having only six months of recent experience will not be much help in landing another. Little guys like me get much less severance pay than management, and there is no pleasant send-off. Usually HR people escort us out of the building like felons, with no opportunity to get our personal things from our cube or computer. Strangers look through our desk drawers and send our personal effects home later.

A fairly easy argument can be made that our Internal Audit department is not fit for purpose. We are not even required by regulations and don't contribute to the bottom line—unless, of course, you consider the savings that will result from my fraud discovery. I will make a rather significant contribution just by closing down the mother-daughter team currently taking millions from that bottom line. My unauthorized work might actually save our department from the grim reaper of HR, or maybe just save me. Clearly I am the cheapest person in the department, which is often how layoff decisions are made. I need to get this fraud discovery in front of Frank and Hal right away so that it has time to float up the chain to those responsible for modifying the existing org charts.

No one from my group is in yet, and I feel ill at the thought of potential unemployment. I wonder about the name "Project Titanic." It amazes me, the time executives spend thinking up code names for their projects. Winston had run a few by me over the years. Once his company was desperately seeking a merger partner, but none of their first choices were interested. When they landed on a target from the second round of possibilities, I recommended it be called Project Jagger, as in you can't always get what you want. Winston loved it, and it stuck. I wonder which brain trust had been tapped to think up this one. "Titanic" is indeed appropriate. Negligence by leadership resulting in harm to the masses, and only the rich would survive. Around a quarter to nine the meeting ends and I disconnect the phone and remove my earbud.

I think about e-mailing Frank or Hal to let them know about the Mazie/Amy caper, but I believe the scheme will be better discussed in person. I think that deep down every one of us auditor types wants to uncover a fraud. Not that we want fraud to occur—we just want to be the ones to discover it. After all, so much of internal audit work is tedious and mind numbing, and the notion that you might identify something worthy of a *Law & Order* episode provides enough incentive to prevent heavy drinking or suicide.

"Frank." I stand up and follow him as he walks past my cube to his office. I stand in his doorway and watch him hang up his jacket and put down his briefcase.

"Can it wait, Tanzie?" he asks. "I haven't even had coffee yet." He sits down at his computer, and I take the hint.

"Can I get you some?" I offer.

"Sure. Creamer and some of the yellow sweetener. Not the pink stuff, okay? And by the way, if you're going to be out more than a day, you need to give a written doctor's note."

"But I didn't go to the doctor, Frank. Are you sure that's policy?"

"It's my policy, Tanzie."

"Right." I seethe as I head to the coffee bar. I work for Hal, not Frank, and besides, I came in on the weekend. I got my work done.

When I return with Frank's coffee, he is on the phone and shoos me out with a dismissive wave and no "thank you."

Mazie has been stealing for about three years; what will a couple more minutes matter? I can always bring it up at the staff meeting. I use the time to go over the accounts payable data. There is no consistent approver on the fraudulent invoices, so I am satisfied that no one else at Bishop is involved in their embezzlement scheme. They must have created the invoices and just forged the approver's signature. It's really the setup person who takes a hard look at an invoice anyway, and that is Amy. The approvers often don't even look at the paperwork. Sometimes they are just too busy and electronically post their approval without ever checking.

A ping on my inbox indicates that the staff meeting has been canceled. I stand up—based on what I heard on the conference call this morning, if I want to keep my job I need to get my bosses working on this fraud investigation immediately—but instead I watch, shocked, as Hal walks by my cube and heads for the elevator bank. I sit down, thinking about what Skip said on the phone: *Our timeline on this is to begin this morning with some top-level items.* If Hal is one of those, I really am one of the "broader elements" on the chopping block. I quickly start to revise my plans.

Hal returns in about thirty minutes or so, and without saying a word he shuts his door with a heavy thud. Moe and Frank both walk out of their offices and look at one another, wondering what it is all about.

"Frank," I call out of my cube, "do you have a minute? I really need to talk to you about something."

"Give me ten minutes," he says and holds up his index finger as he walks with Moe to the men's room, coffee bar, or somewhere else I am not welcome.

Ten minutes takes about thirty, and when the two return, Moe is looking at his iPhone as they go directly into Hal's office and close the door. They come out after a while, close Hal's door behind them, and then leave again together, and I'm alone in my cube. After about an hour, I see Hal leave, briefcase in hand.

"Are you feeling okay?" I ask as Hal walks past. Perhaps my female problems are contagious.

"Nope," he says, and that is it. He doesn't look at me, just keeps going on his way to the elevator.

Frank returns, and I peek around the door and again request some time.

"Okay, come on in," he says, sounding a little irritated. He motions for me to sit in the chair across from his desk.

"Frank, I noticed something odd when I was doing the vendor testing. I did a little digging, and I think there might be some fraudulent expenses being paid out of Accounts Payable. And I think I know who is involved."

"I just did an Accounts Payable audit last year before I was hired at Bishop. Hal engaged Boyd and Associates and I ran that audit. That's how I met Hal. How long do you think this has been going on?" I can tell he is getting defensive.

"I'm not sure—and it is confusing—but I believe at least three years."

"How did you discover this?"

155

"Well, when you had me do the testing, the data dump looked funny. There was really quite a lot of activity, so I ran some pivot tables and the activity stuck out."

"I didn't see that when I reviewed your testing, Tanzie. There were no exceptions noted."

"I know. But that was just a test for approval of new vendors. It was the activity from changes that made me dig a little deeper. I'm sure you would have done the same, Frank. It may not have shown up on your sample when you tested it last year. I probably just got lucky."

This is not entirely true. Often auditors test just a small sample rather than look for anomalies via data analytics, the preferred method. The technique takes more skill, but it is regarded in the profession as superior, particularly when looking for fraudulent transactions. I find it so frustrating to work for bottom-feeders who do not understand the technical side of auditing enough to appreciate someone who does.

"Have you shown this work to anyone else?"

"No, not yet. I wanted to talk with you first. I really think there are two people involved."

"Collusion?" Frank perks up.

"Yes, it's a mother-daughter scheme."

"No auditor is expected to detect fraud in a collusion scheme." Frank looks like he's relaxing a bit. "How did you find this?"

This is the critical moment. On one hand, if I stroke his ego by attributing my discovery to blind luck, there will be no basis for career advancement. On the other hand, if I detail how I spied on Mazie and hacked into her computer, surely I will be accused of poor judgment again. I choose somewhere in the middle. The best strategy might be to include Frank in the discovery. He might be receptive enough to recognize my skills as a huge benefit to his own advancement.

"Frank, if you have some time, let me walk you through how my data analytics work. This was part of that seminar Hal sent me to when I first started. I think you and Moe were out of town," I say, trying not to appear too much of a smarty-pants.

"All right, Tanzie. Show me what you got."

I scoot a guest chair over to Frank's side of the desk and guide him through the process of culling through the minutia of thousands of individual transactions to identify the anomalies that detect fraud. To my surprise, Frank is not only receptive, he seems to appreciate the explanation. It is the first time I feel even a glimmer of respect from my immediate boss. He asks questions, and for once I don't feel the need to feign confusion.

"Tanzie, this is major fraud we've uncovered."

We?

"Yes, I know, Frank," I say. "I know Hal is gone for the day, but maybe we should meet with him about it when he gets back?" I watch Frank to see if I can detect any clues regarding Hal's employment situation in his response.

"I don't think we can wait for that," Frank says as he picks up the receiver and dials a four-digit extension. The phone is on speaker, and after several rings a voice mail greeting comes on.

"Hello. This is Jim Davenport, Chief Compliance Officer for the Bishop Group. I'm away from my desk, but please leave a message and I'll get back to you as soon as possible."

Frank cancels the speaker option when the beep sounds, but he stays on the line. "Jim, this is Frank Singleton in Internal

Audit. I've uncovered a large embezzlement scheme down here and need to discuss our next steps. Please give me a call when you have a minute."

I feel the blood drain from my face, realizing what just happened. *It wasn't even "we" anymore.* "I may need you to help with some of the paperwork after I meet with Jim. I'll give you a call and let you know what I need. That's it for now." He turns his attention to his Outlook screen, and I push my chair back to its original spot, get up, and leave his office without looking back.

I am screaming inside my brain. *So Frank is taking credit for my work. Why am I not surprised?* This is absolutely infuriating. I do not stop by my desk but go straight to the ladies' room to cool down a bit.

As I push open the door, I hear conversation from the stalls, and I very quietly shut the door so that I will not be noticed. The conversation is between two payroll ladies listing the names of the executives who got axed this morning and making the type of snide remarks that clerks make about the higher-ups in any company. But when they get to Hal they are not snide at all.

"Poor Hal. He is such a great guy; I can't believe they let him go," one set of legs says to the other. I quietly leave the main bathroom and wait in the vestibule to collect my thoughts.

So Hal got the boot after all. I figure Moe and Frank know about Hal by now, which explains their closed-door meetings and private talks this morning. There is now a power vacuum, and Frank and Moe will be wondering which of them might be promoted to the Chief Auditor position. What I know and what they don't is that there is a good chance the entire department will be considered "not fit for purpose" and eliminated during the greater layoff yet to be scheduled.

Still, Frank has a sizable advantage thanks to *my* fraud discovery. He can make a compelling argument to keep his job or even get promoted. He might very well decide to keep me too so that he can leverage my skills; but even so, it is clear I won't receive credit or advancement of any kind.

The reality hits me hard. I will never be anything but his helper, a cube dweller with no control or decision-making capability. Frank showed me his true nature this morning, and I would rather starve on the streets than propel his career forward with my abilities. I sit on the little couch in the ladies' room vestibule to evaluate my options. I think about quitting. Just walking into Frank's office and telling him. But what good will that do? Quitting without notice has absolutely no upside other than the momentary satisfaction derived from an immature outburst. "She was unstable," Frank would say to everyone. "Poor thing. Really sort of sad."

Option two is to suck it up and see what happens in the coming days. Maybe I will get laid off, or maybe not. Maybe Frank will stay, maybe Moe, maybe me, or maybe nobody. I don't care anymore.

My pity party is interrupted by the vroom of toilets flushing and the portly payroll ladies emerging from their stalls to wash their hands. I notice the nervous look they give each other, wondering how long I have been sitting there and whether I have overheard their confidential conversation. I need to regroup, and I follow the ladies out and walk back to my cube.

When I get back to my desk, Moe is in Frank's office. I tap on the door.

"I just heard they let Hal go," I tell them.

"Where did you hear that from?" Frank looks perturbed.

The doling out of information in the corporate world has a pre-scribed pecking order, and I have just breached the unspoken rule of finding something out before management told me.

"Ladies' room." *Take that. You boys have your network, but those payroll ladies know all.*

"What else did you hear?" Moe asks. So he thinks I might know something he doesn't.

"Just some other executive names, but I don't know who they are. It was all very confusing." I smile as I leave Frank's office. I am not about to give Frank anything again. Let him meet with Jim in Legal and fumble through information he doesn't fully understand. He will need me eventually, and the next time I will not be quite so willing to work without something for myself.

I grab my jacket from the back of my desk chair and head out for an early lunch. Maybe I won't return at all. What are those two going to do about it? They are probably too focused on their own futures to give me a second thought. When lay-off rumors permeate an organization, all productivity comes to an abrupt halt. People spend days speculating when, who, and how much—how much being the primary issue. Some people would love to be let go and take the package; others are com-pletely torn up about the uncertainty of being unemployed or the stigma of being let go. I wonder which type I am, really.

———◆———

As I walk through the Bishop lobby on my way to the garage, I see Baldwin and a younger man heading out together. The younger man's lightbulb shape marks him as a Bishop, and I wonder if perhaps this is Brandon about to get an earful from

Uncle Baldwin on the sorry state of the maritime segment. They are involved in conversation and don't acknowledge me as they briskly walk by.

"I made reservations at the French Hen," I overhear Baldwin tell his companion. Baldwin's black Cadillac is waiting for him in the front, and I see them get in it as I cross the street on my way to the garage.

With traffic, that gives me about a two-hour window, so I take the opportunity to go to the public library and do more snooping, knowing that Baldwin will not be on his desktop when I hijack it. My login attempt fails, so I try again but get the same result. I remember being bumped from the account yesterday and try not to panic. Obviously Baldwin has changed his password, but I wonder what else he might do. I take a deep breath and think about what to do next. I debate whether I should take a chance and log in as Marla. What if she is eating lunch at her desk? I punch in the familiar numbers on my phone.

"Bishop Group," the cheerful receptionist answers.

"Marla Walters, please," I say.

"Just a moment while I connect you." And with that the line rings over and over until the voice mail message kicks in.

"Brilliant," I congratulate myself. I hang up before the beep and log in to the Diva Lady account.

I scan her inbox looking for anything that involves the Houston explosion. I spot a notice for a meeting at 5:30 that evening with Sullivan and the VP of insurance and risk management. All parties are on-site, so I cannot call in like I did earlier that morning. How I would love to be a fly on the wall in that meeting.

I go to my favorite Utica Square restaurant, which has an attached market that sells specialty meats and gourmet items.

As I munch on my salad, I go over the events of the past days in my mind. In retrospect, they seem crazy. I am starting to get so caught up in this snooping thing that it has become an obsession with me. It is risky, and I love it. It will even be better with Lucy on board.

There have been so few challenges in my life. While I was married to Winston, I devoted my time to bettering my golf game, and that became a twenty-year obsession. I worked at it hard and with laser focus. I was club champion seven years out of ten and the consistent runner-up once Vivian Campbell joined our club. She had played on the women's team at the University of Texas. Young and strong, she could get to the green on some of the par fours on a single drive. She took three days off from her job as an investment banker to play in the club championship every May and kick my ever-growing ass. It sort of foreshadowed my future, being dethroned by a younger woman and all. Still, at that time I had a respectable single-digit handicap and lived for the high that came from competitive golf. Since moving to Tulsa, I have not had anything to challenge me, and this spying stuff brings back those old feelings in a big way.

An idea begins to take shape in my head—suddenly I know how I could spy on the meeting that evening. *Be careful*, I tell myself, knowing I'm probably not going to listen.

CHAPTER TWELVE

After wandering around Wal-Mart for what seems like forever, I find what I need—all for less than $25—and head back to my condo. I change into dark blue Dickies and sneakers, pulling my hair back into a ponytail fastened by a rubber band. I wash the makeup off my face and stare at the dark-eyed frump in the mirror. My pants are tight, given my recent weight gain, and the muffin top peeking out at the sides of my cleaning smock gives me an authentic look. I shove a rag into my back pocket and push the elastic coil holding the office keys up to the middle of my forearm. To the untrained eye, I look exactly like any member of the janitorial staff who roams around the Bishop building after hours and on weekends.

I drive up to the Bishop building against the outbound five o'clock traffic, parking a couple of blocks away. I don't want anybody noticing the cleaning lady getting out of the late model Lexus with Texas plates. My heart is pounding as I get on the elevator. There is still time to back out, but in my mind I am committed.

I get out on thirty, just as the executive administrative assistants are packing up for the day. No one gives me a second look as I take my rag and start to dust the decorative bookcase that flanks the entrance to the executive conference room. I push open the glass door and survey the room, looking for the perfect spot. A decorative bronze of a roughneck with a huge wrench in his hand sits high on a knickknack shelf. Checking to make sure no one is looking, I reach up, place my iPhone behind it, and stand back. This placement allows for fairly good sound reception, and the statue base completely eclipses my device. It is high enough on the shelf and so close to the wall that even the exceptionally tall Bishops could not see it without considerable effort. I am careful to turn my sound off after the near miss with Lucy's text when I was under the desk yesterday.

This is risky, for sure. If my phone were discovered, they would probably find out that it belongs to me, even with its password protection. It occurs to me that they might actually engage Internal Audit to find out who owns the phone, and I smile at the thought. I step back and look around, comfortable with my decision but a little nervous nonetheless. I am absolutely confident that the phone will not be noticed, and my disguise as a cleaning lady is flawless. Unlike yesterday, I have meticulously planned this surveillance and will not be relegated to the underside of a desk.

By 5:30, the floor is deserted except for the general counsel, Baldwin, and Bennet. The elevator dings, and a tall guy with salt-and-pepper hair and a shorter fellow who is completely bald walk past me and down the hall to Baldwin's office. The two return and enter the conference room, where Baldwin, the general counsel, and Bennet join them almost immediately. The doors close. I keep my head down and continue to dust out of earshot of the meeting, knowing that the record feature on my phone is capturing every word. My presence is as noticeable as the fly on the wall I was hoping to be. I silently congratulate myself on my ingenuity.

I wait out the time in the executive ladies' room, taking off my smock in case the real cleaning crew comes by. There are no female executives at Bishop, so there is zero chance of being discovered by anyone. I am getting bored after the first hour and decide to emerge for a quick look. With my smock back on, I walk casually by the conference room. All parties are still in deep discussion. I can't make out the words through the glass, but the tone sounds hostile to say the least. So it's back to the bathroom again, where I sit and wait some more. At one point I climb onto a toilet to see if I can hear anything through the exhaust fan, but no dice. When I put my ear to the wall I hear nothing.

Around 7:30 I venture out again. The main lights are still on, and I make my way to the executive coffee bar for a change of scenery. I decide to wash out the coffee pot just to have something to do. I jump at the sound of footsteps headed my way as I am drying the green-handled carafe, but manage to stay calm and in character when in walks the short bald man. He abruptly takes the coffee pot out of my hands and begins to make a fresh pot, opening and closing drawers before finding the Starbucks bag, which he opens and pours into the paper filter. I find a spray bottle under the sink and begin to clean tabletops while the man waits for his coffee to brew. To my amazement, he never acknowledges me or makes eye contact. My heart pounds and I'm sweating again, but the man doesn't notice. I am a nobody. Perfect.

A moment later, the salt-and-pepper-haired man comes in. He grabs a blue Bishop-logoed mug from the cupboard above the coffeemaker.

"It's going to be a long fucking night, Sully," he complains to the bald man.

The salt-and-pepper-haired man removes the coffee pot mid-cycle and fills his mug, sending a steady stream of coffee from the coffeemaker splattering onto the burner, onto the counter, and then to the floor.

"Shit!" he yells, jumping back. Instead of putting the pot back to stop the flow, he pours Sully a cup and then shoves the pot back into the brewer with an angry slam. Both men leave the break room, stepping over the mess they have left for me to clean up.

After I clean up the coffee, I retreat to the ladies' room to continue the waiting game. I stay put for another hour or so, killing time reading a day-old *Wall Street Journal* retrieved from the coffee bar trash can. I continue to periodically sneak out of the bathroom to see if the meeting is still going on, worrying that my phone battery will die or that the meeting will go on past ten and interfere with my plans for picking up Lucy later tonight.

Around 9:15, I can tell the meeting is breaking up, and I guess only Bennet and Baldwin remain in the conference room because I hear the other two men talking as they get on the elevator. I wait another twenty minutes or so before I come out from hiding in the restroom to find them gone and the conference room dark. I can hear the vacuums of the real janitors, but they take no notice of me as I enter the conference room to retrieve my phone. I quickly board the elevator and get out of Dodge.

Alone in the elevator, I tear off my smock and cram it into my purse. As calm as I was during my reconnaissance, I begin to shake at the enormity of what I have just done. I took a huge risk but came out on top for the first time in a while. In the past few days I have been on an emotional roller coaster. Excitement, sorrow, betrayal—but the feeling I have at this moment is of power and success. I never want it to end.

By the time I get to my car I am having trouble controlling myself. I do a victory dance before I get in. I can't wait for Lucy to arrive so she can share the euphoria. It has been a long time coming.

My phone battery is just about spent, so I can't listen to the whole meeting until I charge the phone, and even with all my meticulous planning, I have forgotten to bring my charger with me. My incredible high continues as I drive back to my condo, plug in my phone, and head out to my balcony for a celebratory smoke. No glass of wine this time, since I have to stay up late and drive to the airport. With just about four hours of recorded conversation, I elect to wait until Lucy arrives so we can listen together.

I scarf down a microwaved frozen meal and head to the Tulsa International Airport. There is nothing international about the Tulsa airport unless you consider Texas a foreign country, which many Okies do. I have been told that the international refers to private plane facilities, which, unlike the commercial carriers, fly in from Canada or Mexico and require a customs representative upon arrival.

I haven't seen Lucy in a couple years, but she hasn't changed a bit. She's tall and slim with flaming red curls that fall almost to her waist and the perky bust line of a woman half her age. From the back she looks like she could be twenty-five; from the front, while it is clear she is no teenager, she does not look at all like a fifty-three-ish farmer who spends most of her time in the sun herding sheep and cultivating organic crops. Lucy wears no makeup and has not a single gray hair to cover up with product. She's extremely fit from her active lifestyle and is one of those timeless beauties who are attractive at any age. Once again, I find myself in the presence of someone who looks much better than I, and it makes me momentarily jealous.

"Tanzie! Good to see you!" Lucy squeals as she gets in the passenger seat. She lives in jeans and has carried only a backpack for her two-night stay.

"You've put on some weight, Tanzie. You really need to come stay with me. I'll get you in shape!"

"Thanks, Lucy. I know."

"You don't look bad. It is just sort of shocking, that's all. You'll always be my beautiful little sister. You know that."

"Would you like to go get something to eat?"

"No thanks. I had a three-hour layover in Houston and was surprised at some of the eating choices available. I ate at a little organic place in Terminal E." No, Lucy would never think of sneaking into the airport lounge like her devious sister.

"Tired?"

"Yeah. I am. I had to get up really early to drive through San Francisco to catch the flight."

I tell Lucy about the meeting and she roars with laughter. "You, the society dame, a janitor? I can't believe it. Now I see where Lulu gets her acting talent!"

"Well, it worked."

"I love it Tanzie. I told you this would be an adventure. Who will you be next time? A security guard?"

"That's an idea. Maybe."

We head back to my condo and I uncork a bottle of red wine from a winery founded by a couple of Lucy's friends in Yountville.

"Oh, how thoughtful, Tanzie, thank you."

"I'm excited you're here, Lucy." We clink our glasses and I fill Lucy in on the fraud, Frank, my hopeless career, and the layoffs. Lucy stifles a yawn, and I can tell she can hardly keep her eyes open.

"I really should be depressed, but somehow I'm relieved," I say. "I'm really happy. Tonight was a blast. It really was."

"Let's listen to the tape, Tanzie, or go through the files. Let's get going on this," Lucy suggests, trying to muster a second wind.

"Okay."

I refill our glasses and walk over to retrieve my purse from the bedroom. I take a moment to change into my jammies and get more comfortable. When I return to the living room, Lucy is asleep. I don't have the heart to wake her, so I take off her glasses, cover her with a blanket, and prop a down pillow next to her head. I kiss my sister on the forehead and turn out the light, relieved that now I can also rest. It has been an exhausting day.

I try to be quiet when I get up to make the coffee, but Lucy, who is still asleep on the sofa, stirs and puts on her glasses.

"Good morning."

"Hi. How did you sleep?"

"Fine, actually. This couch is pretty comfortable for an old gal like me."

"You look great, Lucy. I swear you never age. Coffee?" I know she doesn't drink coffee, but thought I'd ask her anyway.

"I like wheat grass. Got any? Or maybe some herbal tea?"

Knowing Lucy was coming, I had shopped for her type of eats: organic kale, free-range eggs, and yes, herbal tea, but no wheat grass.

"Chamomile okay? Or I have something here called Red Zinger."

"Ooooh. Red Zinger, please."

I don't want Lucy to know I smoke, so I had decided not to while she is staying with me. I know it's lame, but I'm private about my character flaws. I put the kettle on and head to my room to get dressed and leave the bathroom for Lucy.

"That's a cute outfit, Tanzie," she says about the slacks and blazer I'd bought in Houston.

"Thanks."

Sometime in the night, Lucy had changed into a nightshirt made from green cotton she had grown, spun, and then woven herself. It did not do her beauty justice, but that is so Lucy. She never gives her looks a second thought. She is consumed with saving the planet and takes every single tiny decision she makes in a day very seriously, mindful of its impact on the earth's sustainability. I hand her the mug of bright red hibiscus tea.

"Are you going in to work today?" she asks.

"Yeah. But not all day. I should be home a little after noon or so. The flash drive with the files I took from Baldwin's secretary is on my computer. Maybe you could take a look at them while I'm gone. I'm thinking we should divide and conquer to make maximum use of our time."

"So you used your phone? Clever. I didn't know you could do that with an iPhone. Is it an app?"

"Nope. It's just part of the utility function. Pretty amazing. I wonder how many people know they are being recorded. It's a pretty common thing to have someone's phone lying on the table during a meeting. Lucy, I'll take notes on the meeting and you take notes on the files. We can get together later and debrief each other on what we've found."

"Sounds like a plan, Tanzie."

"Yep, it's a plan," I say, taking a sip of coffee.

"Tanzie, you seem so great. I haven't seen you like this since we were kids." She hesitates before continuing. "I don't want to dwell on painful memories, but I think the divorce has been good for you. You're like your own person again. Maybe it's a good thing that your career is going in the toilet. Why would you ever think of settling for a career at Bishop, of all things? You're so much better than that."

"I think you may be right, Lucy. I think you may be right."

CHAPTER THIRTEEN

I arrive at my desk and plug in my earbuds after settling with a cup of Best Java coffee. Four hours is going to be a long time to listen, but there doesn't seem to be much going on in my department at the moment other than speculation about layoffs.

I listen to the beginning of the meeting, and the sound is remarkably clear. It seems like the beginning of most executive meetings. I had some experience with these back in my old career days. Baldwin opens with a "Thank you all for making time for this very crucial topic." Sullivan brings the group up to speed on LEAR_2008_17_Houston_Gas.

"Best I can tell," Sullivan says, "the pipeline that ruptured was laid in the early '30s, made of cast iron before cathodic protection was required to inhibit rust. Back then it was sort of an anything-goes sort of thing. It also appears that a slightly larger pipe was used for that section rather than the thirty-inch pipe that was used for the rest of the pipeline."

"Why is that?" asks an unfamiliar voice.

"Well, we don't know. Probably they ran out of the thirty inch and had some other material lying around. Or maybe there was some pipe they initially rejected but decided to use in a pinch. In the interest of time, they may have used what they had rather than delay the project waiting for a materials shipment. You folks need to understand—it was a different world back then. No regulations or fines. Plus, back then this pipeline was in the middle of nowhere. Nothing but cow pasture and rice fields . . . Anyway, when we did our routine pigging, the results were not precise for that particular segment. That section had some variability in the wall thickness, but that could have been due to the difference in pipe size or slight corrosion. We just didn't have very good information at the time. That said, we did notice some corrosion and faulty welds upstream near Lockhart, and we replaced several sections in 2009."

"So why didn't we do more testing on the Houston segment?" This must be the insurance executive talking, the salt-and-pepper-haired charmer from last night.

"A few reasons. First of all, that Houston segment had all kinds of improvements on top of it—houses, retail, that sort of thing. Second, we were not entirely sure where the pipeline was."

"You're kidding me. How is that possible?" This is Bennet asking the questions now.

"If you recall, Bennet, we didn't construct this pipeline. It had five different owners before we got it in 1998, and the mapping and right-of-way files were not complete. This is not an easy thing to do, to figure out where the pipe was laid, and it would have required millions to excavate and lots of time, too. This is a major residential area. Anyway, Wagner Jones was in the process of putting a project together in '09 to determine the best course of action when he got sick and retired. The whole thing just fell through the cracks, what with the Kansas crude spill when I transferred into the department."

"So do you think we can be found negligent?"

"The DOT and PHSMA regs are pretty clear about required documentation and maintenance protocol. I think they would find us in violation of their protocols, but whether that means we have been negligent is more of a legal term. I can't really answer that."

"So do we have updated casualty figures?" Baldwin asks.

"Right now it's fifty-three dead and seventy-seven injured, but some of those injured may not make it. The max looks like it's in the neighborhood of fifty-eight or sixty." This was the insurance executive talking again.

"Judas Priest, Sullivan! How did you let this happen? All those people dead, families ruined—"

"Do we have damage estimates?" a calmer Bennet interrupts.

"Not exactly, but oil and gas is not a popular industry right now. Add to that the fact that these folks in Houston were wealthy and had long years of earning big money ahead of them. Bill Matheson is handling a few of the cases, and we all know what he's like."

"Can we shift blame somehow? To terrorism, maybe? And what about all those construction crews; they've been digging around there for years. How sure are we that they didn't cause this?"

"The exact cause has not been established yet, but under these circumstances, we may want to discuss some strategies to pull out of our you-know-whats, if and when the time comes."

I think it's funny that the salt-and-pepper-haired man is so careful with his language in front of the Bishops, in contrast to his coffee bar vulgarity last night.

"We can file some preemptive motions as early as tomorrow if you like," begins another unfamiliar voice that I suspect is the general counsel. "I can get Josh working on that over at Schwab & Middleton. We should also see about securing settlements from as many people as we can early on. Even if it is not our fault, you can be sure we will be involved in damage suits. The sooner we can get in front of this, the better."

"Good. I like that," a composed Baldwin weighs in.

The meeting goes on for hours. It is clear that there was not intentional disregard for maintenance, but rather embarrassment at the incompetence that had let something so important fall off the radar. There is endless discussion involving how accurate the testing information was and more about the specifics of the pipe design, who knew what and what decisions had been made and by whom, what insurance covered and what it did not. Baldwin insisted that all copies of the LEAR and related emails be deleted immediately. So for certain, now, I have the only one.

"What do we do now?" Bennet asks at around hour three.

"The way I see it," begins the general counsel, "if this thing turns out to be related to a maintenance issue, we'll have sizable liability. No question about that. The damages will likely exceed our insurance, and they are difficult to quantify this early. The casualties are people with the means to tie us up in court for a good deal of time. But what I do know is that if you cover this thing up, Bennet, you run the risk that it leaks out, and then that really is the end for all of us. If fraud is established, the insurance companies could yell foul and not pay, the Justice Department would be here shutting you down, and we'll be sharing a cell with Jeff Skilling. Remember Enron?"

"I did not spend the last thirty years of my life building all this up to be taken down by some incompetent nitwit in my environmental group!" This sounds like Baldwin, and the nitwit he means is probably Sullivan. This is finally getting good.

More discussion about what needs to be deleted and what should be kept continues for a while and then winds down to silence. The general counsel gets nowhere when he cautions the group not to destroy anything, as subpoenas have been received from the DOT, EPA, and several other agencies already. Both Baldwin and Bennet are adamant that any documentation illuminating the fact that they knew about corrosion in the Houston pipeline system should be gone.

"Thank you for your time, gentlemen." And I hear the scrape of chairs as the non-Bishops leave the meeting.

Next, I hear a few minutes of dead air, and I envision the two brothers staring at each other.

"What worries me most about all of this, Baldwin, is our credit tightening."

My mouth drops open in my cube, and I quickly close it. *Oh my God. I haven't even thought of that. I really am stale. All this time the conversation has been about fines, when the true risk to the Bishop Group is the impact on their trading operation.*

While some of Bishop's revenue comes from fees for storing or moving product, a more significant slice is from their trading and marketing arm. In the simplest of terms, it is gambling on the price of commodities. I make a deal to sell you a barrel of oil next month for $100. If the price on the open market next month is $95, then I make $5; if the price next month is $105, then I lose $5. Extend those deals out for years and for huge volumes, and the profits and losses become enormous. While there is certainly risk involved, the potential profits are hard to resist.

The best returns in trading operations are derived from companies with exceptional credit ratings—in other words, companies to whom lenders extend a large credit line and who aren't required to post margin or give a cash deposit as a guarantee that they will make good on a bad bet. It is like a poker game. The casinos extend credit to people with adequate net worth to cover their debts. When credit gets tight or a company falls in their credit rating, their trading partners can immediately reduce the credit line and demand payment for any outstanding amount over that reduced limit and require them to post margin, which can consume cash quickly and leave them without enough to fund their operations. Lawsuits can drag on for years, but credit tightening in an energy-trading arena can topple a huge company overnight.

Right now, Bishop has an exceptional credit rating. If news of their complicity in the pipeline is revealed, that could change.

"The banks just aren't lending right now," Bennet says. "The last thing we need is a credit squeeze. First one guy wants us to post margin, then the others find out and want it too. Pretty soon it dominoes and we have no cash at all."

"Bennet, are you telling me we are over our heads on the trading floor?" Baldwin sounds nervous. Since Baldwin is the Chief Operating Officer, his focus is on the mundane tasks of making the plants run and the pipelines flow—the physical business. He might not have much visibility into the less tangible side of trading derivatives.

"No no," says Bennet. "I'm saying that this Houston catastrophe could be more than just jury awards, fines, and court fees. It could affect our credit, which has enormous impact on the marketing and trading operations. If not handled correctly, it could kill us. We really need to make sure that bad press is minimized and judgments are contained."

Again there is silence.

"What if we went to one of the Houston sewer contractors and, say, offered them some incentive to admit liability? What's bankruptcy to them if they come out with a personal $50 million or so? If the city of Houston is involved as a co-litigant, we may be able to save a ton on this," Baldwin suggests.

"Do you have any contacts down there?"

"Absolutely. I have contacts everywhere, Benny."

"This may have legs, but let's just keep that between us, if you know what I mean."

Their conversation shifts to family stuff and late dinner plans. I look at my watch, and it is past two.

I am just about to call Lucy on my cell when my desk phone rings.

"This is Skip Perkinson, Tanzie. I'm in here with Frank. I'm wondering if you could come to my office on twenty-nine."

I swallow deeply. "Of course. Do I need to bring anything?" I ask, trying to stay calm. Surely if I am about to be fired, it would not be by the head of HR. More likely a perky junior representative would have that unpleasant task. "Skip, I don't think I have the right badge to get onto the twenty-ninth floor. It will take me a minute to get a security escort." I can use my janitor badge, of course, but I'm not about to let him know that.

"I'll send Carol, my admin, to meet you in the lobby," Skip says.

This ride up to twenty-nine is nothing like the one with Keith the security guard. Carol is the typical adorable blonde who resides in almost every HR department, with trendy clothes and accessories. She is chatty and I try to remain very calm. Have they discovered that I hacked Baldwin's computer, or that I broke in last night, or that I dialed into the executive meeting? I take deep breaths and smile at Carol's inane banter until she delivers me to Skip.

Frank sits at a mahogany conference table with his laptop open and does not get up like Skip does when I enter the room.

"Have a seat, Tanzie." Skip gestures to a chair next to Frank, who is consumed with his computer screen and doesn't even make eye contact as I sit down.

"What can I do for you?" I ask Skip as I look at Frank's screen to get some idea as to why I have been summoned.

"Frank tells me that he has uncovered a rather sophisticated embezzlement ring in our Accounts Payable department, and he indicated that you might be able to put some documentation together for us." Accounts payable fraud has all the sophistication of a corndog. It's common stuff, but I suppose Frank has built it up to make himself look like a mastermind.

I take my first full exhale since I picked up the phone. I am so relieved about not being sacked that I forget to be pissed at Frank for once again taking credit for my discovery.

"Frank mentioned that it's a mother-daughter duo, but he has been unable to give me their names so that we can do an investigation on our end," Skip continues. I suppress a chuckle. How embarrassing for poor Frank to have met with the head of HR to crow about his discovery, only to realize that he never asked me the names of the employees responsible, and that his computer skills are so poor that he can't even repeat what I showed him in his office yesterday.

I bring Skip up to speed, outlining how the fraud works and giving Mazie's and Amy's full names.

"Good work," Skip says. "Jim is out this week, but I think we need to put together some documentation to put in front of him when he returns on Monday,"

"Why can't you just fire them?" I ask.

"If only it were that easy, Tanzie. We need to get paperwork in order. Legal will need to weigh in, and we will probably need to get in front of Bennet or Baldwin. And they're pretty tied up at the moment. We open ourselves up to litigation if we don't have every i dotted and t crossed on this."

"I see. So they just continue doing what they do until we can get all the paperwork and approvals in order? That doesn't seem right."

I can feel Frank glaring at me. Imagine, questioning the great Skip Perkinson instead of just executing the task I was given!

"Sadly, yes, Tanzie," Skip continues. "What I need from you and Frank is a write-up in layman's terms about what has gone on, by whom, and for how long. We'll also need some sort of estimate as to the amount stolen. Do you think you can have that to me by Monday morning?"

Skip looks at Frank and Frank looks at me. Actually, I can have it done in an hour, but I see no reason to rush on this since nothing is going to be done until Monday.

"Yes, of course."

"That won't be a problem, Skip," Frank interrupts as he shuts his computer and stands up to shake Skip's hand. He is taking over once again, but I can tell that Skip knows what is really going on.

Carol escorts Frank and me to the elevators and we ride down in silence. When we arrive back on six, Frank stands by my cube. I wait for an apology, but he never offers one.

"Tanzie, have that documentation to me by Friday morning so I have a chance to review it."

"Sure thing, Frank." I know he wants it so he can email it himself to Jim and Skip, hoping against hope that he can then recover from his lapse in front of Skip today. One thing is certain, though: If Frank stays, I will be kept on. It is clear he needs me. It is also a definite possibility that Skip, who surely is responsible for the reorg, has noticed that I am much sharper than Frank and will keep me on board. Suddenly, things are looking up.

call Lucy but she doesn't pick up, so I spend the next hour or so replaying the tape, making notes on the times at which the most damaging conversations took place. It is that fraud triangle all over again. The extreme *pressure* of possibly losing their company and the personal humiliation for having let all those people die; the *opportunity* to make it all go away by greasing the palm of a Houston sewer contracting firm president; and the *rationalization* that it isn't really the Bishops' fault but in fact the nitwit in EH&S who dropped the ball.

This gives me an interesting view into how these guys think. There is no discussion of why EH&S was so thinly staffed in the first place that they could not properly deal with the many issues they had on their plate. I feel bad for poor Sullivan; he is the internal scapegoat here. I suspect that he will meet the same fate as good old Hal, unless they keep him on board just to keep his mouth shut.

It is not uncommon for people caught up in a major problem to make the problem bigger with a cover-up. In this case, if Bishop's general counsel was correct, the brothers might have to pay out huge damages, maybe even sell off a business unit or two and make some changes to their trading portfolio, but Bishop as a whole could live to fight another day. If they destroyed the paperwork, the Department of Justice could shut them down á la Arthur Andersen. If they bribed a construction firm or sewer contractor in Houston to take the rap, they could go to jail. The cover-up here seemed like a huge mistake; the very hubris that built the Bishop empire could likely serve to destroy it.

There is just something about people who cannot admit mistakes or defeat. Urging them to be reasonable is like trying to teach a pig to sing: They are just incapable.

I once attended a business ethics seminar where it was suggested that when struggling to decide what to do, always imagine your mother or some other loved one is reading about your decision in the newspaper. A company that lets a maintenance project fall through the cracks is just incompetent and possibly criminally negligent. But one that commits fraud by destroying evidence or bribing is in another category. *What would Mama Bishop think of these boys now?* I wonder.

I prepare a summary of events to help with my debrief after work with Lucy. It is true that Bishop did not maintain the section of pipe under the Galleria area. They also did not have adequate records. Those items would be violations of regulatory requirements. However, the actual cause of the explosion and whether Baldwin would in fact bribe someone to take the fall for Bishop are still unknowns. The impact on Bishop's credit and how that will affect the operations going forward is another unknown.

My inclination is to lay low and take my time investigating. As long as I continue to be an employee, I have greater access to information than someone on the outside. Lucy, with her activist viewpoint, will probably want to go screaming to the media about the Bishops. It is probably not a good idea for me to let her know about the bribe possibility just yet. Just as with Mazie and Amy, the longer an investigation goes on behind the scenes, the better the quality of the information gathered will be. I don't like deceiving my sister, but I need to be careful to rein in her enthusiasm for bringing down the Bishops on an uncomfortably accelerated timeline. Lucy might very well be the smarter one, but what I lack in smarts I make up for in strategy and patience.

———◆———

Walking down the hallway leading to my condo, I am surprised to hear Lucy's muffled laughter. I haven't turned the key all the way when Lucy opens the door from the inside.

"She's home," my sister calls over her shoulder to my elusive neighbors Kim and Dan, who are currently sitting in my living room.

Kim and Dan have the three-bedroom unit next to mine, and just after I moved in they occasionally invited me over for a glass of wine or dinner. Dan writes for the *Tulsa World* newspaper and considers himself an oracle of liberal intelligence. He told me one time that he hoped his editorials would, over time, infiltrate the Tea Party brains that controlled Tulsa politics. He is short and has that fortyish receding hairline that signals the transition into middle age for some men. Kim is a trust fund kid from old Tulsa money that allows the couple to live in their swank condo in the most prestigious part of town. I'm only renting my unit, but I understood theirs had cost over $1 million, a gigantic sum considering the affordability of most Tulsa real estate.

Kim is something of an artist and spends her days at her loom weaving tapestry pieces or at her downtown glass-blowing studio. She looks younger than Dan, petite with a few gray strands starting to streak her dark curly hair. Her clothes are comfortable yet chic, and except for the gorgeous platinum, art deco diamond ring she wears on her right hand, no one would ever assume she has the kind of money that supports their comfortable lifestyle.

Ours was one of those friendships you make when you first move to a place. They feel sorry for you and try to include you socially, but after a while, there is really no need on their part to perpetuate the friendship, and the relationship remains friendly but never becomes a close one.

Kim and Dan are active members of the Democratic Party, which has zero clout in Tulsa, or in Oklahoma, for that matter. I think they were at first intrigued by my growing up in the San Francisco Bay Area but less endeared by my choice of workplace. Bishop stands for everything they are against, and I suppose I'm guilty by association. So slowly but steadily I stopped getting invited over for dinner, and they never seemed available to accept the invitations I extended.

"You never told me that Lucy O'Leary is your sister," Kim says as she pours a glass of my zinfandel. "I've been ordering yarn from her and following her environmental initiatives for years. She's my hero."

I go to pour myself a glass, but the bottle is empty. "I'll get another," I say as I walk to the wine rack, grabbing the Ridge and heading to the kitchen.

"I ran into Lucy as she was walking back from Utica Square this afternoon. I recognized her right away; she's pretty unmistakable with that hair. I hope it's okay that we just invited ourselves over."

I should have known that my neighbors would be Lucy fans.

"Not at all," I lie through my country club smile. *I'm not at all ticked that you pretty much wrote me off after a couple of dinners and now pretend like we're best friends when my semi-famous sister appears.*

I had hoped to spend the evening going through the Bishop files with Lucy, not making small talk with the neighbors. I bring the bottle over to the coffee table and place it next to the empty one.

"You didn't tell me your neighbor Dan writes for the *Tulsa World*, Tanzie," Lucy says and smiles knowingly.

"What's happening at Bishop?" Dan asks as I scoot a decorative chair over to the conversation area. I don't really want to squeeze in between Lucy and Kim on the couch.

"I'm not allowed to talk about it." I look at Lucy, who is biting the interior of her cheek to keep her expression in check. Surely she hasn't told them what we are up to.

"Well, I've had it up to here with these goddamn oil companies and their total disregard for the environment and people," Kim begins.

"Pipelines are the safest method of transporting natural gas and crude," I say, sounding like Buster, my talkative friend from the airport. Normally, I take the other side of the argument, but I am still feeling irritated with my neighbors.

"Oh, come on, Tanzie," Lucy says, rolling her eyes. "You know as well as I do that they cut every corner possible to save money, then say any kind of nonsense when they get caught with their pants down." Lucy raises an eyebrow, and I wonder if she has been discussing her purpose for visiting Tulsa with reporter Dan. The three nod their collective left-wing heads as I take a sip of wine and glare at Lucy, hoping she will get the message to keep her mouth shut like she promised.

"Our economy is going to shit right now, and you want to raise the price of power? Who is going to pay for that? What will happen to the elderly and poor when the price of fuel skyrockets? What's your solution?" I ask.

This is directed at Kim and Dan. I know Lucy's solution: go back to the Stone Age. Lucy lives off the grid using solar panels to generate her tiny kilowatt consumption. She drives a Prius but somehow forgets that the electricity is generated by a combined cycle power plant that uses natural gas. She prefers to think that the electricity her vehicle uses has miraculously arrived via the wind turbines that only make economic sense because they suck huge subsidies from the federal government. Lucy is the type of extremist who lives by principles without any consideration for practicality. This is the very attribute I need to manage lest she blow the whole Bishop investigation with her zealotry.

"Here's what I think," Dan begins calmly. "We need to transition from fossil fuels to renewables. Yes, they are more expensive, but what is the true cost of our current system when you factor in the cost of environmental leaks and blowing up innocent people?"

"Well said," injects Lucy. "True cost is an interesting concept. We tend to look at this entirely the wrong way. We never factor in the cost to our planet and people's health when we talk about how cheap fossil fuels are. When you consider the cost of global warning and climate change, it becomes much more expensive. People also forget that our federal government invested heavily in the oil and gas infrastructure back in the mid-1900s through tax incentives and other subsidies. Does anyone ever ask what we could have used that tax money for? Better schools, better research?"

"Enough," I say and get up, heading for the kitchen. I've heard Lucy's rants a million times before. "I'm starving," I say as I open my refrigerator. "Let me throw something together for dinner. How does a kale omelet sound?" I ask, hoping Dan and Kim will take the hint and go back to their place.

"Let's walk over to Flemings," Dan suggests.

"My treat," Kim adds. "I'm so excited to get to talk with Lucy. This is really a thrill."

"Flemings?" Lucy questions. "What kind of food is that, Kim?"

Ah yes. I can predict the next set of questions. Is it organic? Grass fed? Sustainable? Ethically killed? Free range? The list will go on and on until restaurant choices are limited to almost nothing. "We can go somewhere else," Kim suggests.

"Flemings has grass-fed organic lamb on the menu. I was there last week and the waiter pointed it out," Dan injects.

"Is that okay, Lucy? Or do we need to establish the means of death as well? Did the lamb go peacefully, Dan?" I kid.

"Ha ha, Tanzie," Lucy glares. "We do have some work to do, though. Are you sure we have time to go out?"

"We won't make it a long night," Kim pleads.

Lucy looks at me for help, but suddenly saddling my neighbors with a large dinner tab seems like justice for having my evening interrupted.

"Oh, come on, Lucy," I say. "Don't be such a stick in the mud. I skipped lunch and I'm hungry." Besides, I am starting to wonder how much I should share with Lucy about this morning's meeting, and I don't want to have that conversation on an empty stomach.

I am feeling hot again, and catching sight of myself in the mirror, I notice my neck is red. I excuse myself, retreat to my bedroom, and step out onto my balcony to cool down. A front is blowing in, and the night air has a strong bite perfect for my rising temperature. It occurs to me that maybe global warming is caused not by CO_2 emissions but by the increase in menopausal women standing outside.

In total disregard of my promise not to smoke while Lucy is visiting, I light up my cigarette and reflect on my behavior in the living room. Why am I taking Bishop's side on this? I need to calm down and collect myself before I am downright rude, particularly to Lucy, who has traveled so far to help me snoop on the very company I now seem to be defending. I freshen up in the bathroom with a quick gargle and brush of my hair. When I return to the living room, Lucy is collecting the empty wine glasses, alone.

"Where'd they go?" I ask.

"They just went to grab their coats. I don't know why you feel like going out. We need to go over your files. What did you find out about the meeting?"

"There were some interesting discussions. Did you find anything of interest on the flash drive?" I ask, diverting the conversation away from my work.

"Oh, yes indeed. That's why I wanted to blow off dinner. But no. You insisted. And Tanzie—if I were you, I would stop defending those creeps you work for and give serious thought to getting out of there."

"Really? You didn't say anything to Dan about what we're doing, did you?"

There is a tap at the door indicating Dan and Kim are ready to go.

"Don't say anything about this. Okay?" I say, and then I open the door. Lucy grabs her shawl.

"Are you going to be warm enough?" I ask. "I can lend you something."

"Oh no. This wool has been specifically spun for optimum warmth. It is from my sheep. Do you like it?"

"It's lovely," Kim says as she fingers the material, and with that the two textile queens walk ahead, leaving me next to Dan.

We get to the restaurant, and the hostess acts like my neighbors are family. We are seated at a prime table in a quiet, almost private room with floor-to-ceiling wine racks and a lovely fire with an antique rosewood surround. I grab the spot farthest from the fire, knowing that I am cultivating my own warmth this evening. Lucy orders the grass-fed organic lamb from Colorado, naturally, and the rest of us order filets medium rare. My irritation from earlier dissolves; it is fun to go out with people, and I feel my mood shift into friendlier territory. I take a piece of warm bread and slather it with butter. It is actually great to eat with people who are not calculating every calorie in their heads.

"So, I know you can't talk about Bishop's involvement in the Houston explosion," Dan begins, "but how is the climate among the employees?"

"I think it's every man for himself," I say. "The employees are more worried about a layoff than about the poor Houstonians who lived above our pipeline. My boss got canned today."

"Really?" Dan asks, suddenly excited. "Do you think he might be open to being a confidential source for me? Do you think I could contact him?"

Lucy's eyebrow goes up again, and I wonder if she has already assumed just such a role.

"God, no," I say. "Are you kidding? Hal is a company guy."

"Even better," Dan adds. "Those are the best ones. They give their lives to a company and then are let go. They usually know a lot about what is going on, and they are very well connected. Guys like that and jilted girlfriends make incredible sources."

"How do you become a confidential source?" I ask. "Can you remain anonymous, like Deep Throat?"

Lucy gives me a wide-eyed look.

"Hypothetically," I emphasize.

"You can be a confidential source," Dan says, "where someone like you tells me something in confidence, and I go to jail rather than reveal your identity when put on the stand. Or you can be an anonymous source, which means that I never know who is giving me the information. Anonymous sources can be tricky, because unless someone else can validate the information, newspapers are reluctant to print it. That being said, with Internet news, all the lines have blurred a bit." Dan's tone is more engaged than it was during earlier discussions.

"You mean like WikiLeaks?" Lucy asks.

"What if the information is obtained illegally?" I interrupt. "Like through hacking or something?"

"Well, as a reporter, how information was obtained doesn't really matter to me," Dan says. "I just need to know that it is factual. Now, let's get back to your boss, Tanzie. Do you know if he has any useful information, or if he might be mad enough for an interview?"

"You could call him," I say, "but I'm betting his severance agreement probably had language prohibiting him from making defamatory remarks about Bishop. That's pretty standard."

"Do you think it would be unethical to hack into Bishop and find out if they are hiding anything?" Kim asks.

I glance at Lucy. "Are you asking me if I'd do something like that?" I ask Kim.

"No. Not really," she says. "I'm just saying that if these guys are so evil, a person might be justified in stealing information. You could go to the EPA, be a whistle-blower."

"I don't think you can do that if the information is illegally obtained," I reply. "You also can't use information that is subject to attorney-client privilege. My department reports through Legal, so I wouldn't be able to do anything like that. But that's an interesting question, Kim. If you were able to hack into the Bishop email and files and find out what was really going on, would you do it?" I ask the group.

Lucy speaks first. "I think it's your moral responsibility to hack if you can." *Of course you do, Lucy. No surprise there.*

"Would anyone find out?" Kim asks, playing along.

"Nope. Not if you were careful about how you did it," I reply.

"You should be willing to go to jail for it," Lucy adds. "I would want to go to great lengths to make sure that Bishop isn't hiding anything. And furthermore, I would proudly go to jail to prove the point about how evil oil and gas companies are."

Actually, you might be visiting me in jail, I think, and I will not be proud. I will be horrified.

Lucy opens her mouth to continue, but Kim interrupts.

"Okay. I haven't told any of you this—well, except for Dan, of course," she says, giving Dan a loving squeeze. "But my grandfather made a fortune in oil and gas, and our foundation provides early education to low-income Tulsa children. Our family is committed to bettering the world."

Lucy turns to her new friends, eyes narrowed. "Are you willing to give all of what you have to make up for benefiting from your family's exploitation of the country's natural resources?" she asks. "Your family may be giving back, but you're still retaining just enough to ensure your family's financial independence. You still have blood on your hands."

Finally, I think, the extremist surfaces. I can see Kim wince, not realizing that her idol could punch her where it hurts. Surprisingly, I feel a little sorry for her.

"All right, Lucy," I interrupt, "this bullshit that the entire oil and gas industry is inherently evil is crazy. You can't expect people to go back to the dark ages. My personal wealth is also a direct result of the oil and gas business, and I certainly am not willing to donate it all to the Sierra Club for some guilt that I do not share with you. I see a huge difference in the way companies in the industry operate. There are responsible ones, and there are others who cut every corner possible to inflate their bottom line and put communities and the environment at risk when they do so. I don't think you can put everyone in the same pot."

"Of course you don't think that, Tanzie," Lucy spouts in the condescending tone that older sisters reserve for their younger siblings.

"Well, I see it as a matter of degrees, too," Dan chimes in, trying to squelch the hostility. He must be from a small family, I surmise from his desire to become the peacemaker. Big families in general, and big Greek families in particular, tend to argue to the death. It can seem mean to outsiders who grew up in more polite households. But it really just demonstrates how close Lucy and I are: We can yell at each other and neither of us takes it personally. And honestly, the truth is that Lucy and I agree that Bishop has done wrong and should be brought to justice. We just disagree on the methodology, timing, and whether my going to jail should be part of the process.

"Some companies are more responsible than others," Dan continues. "But Bishop is such a classic fuckup." Kim gives Dan a look. "Sorry, Kim, but you know what I mean. They give the entire industry a bad name. Bishop has always been the poster child of doing the bare minimum and skirting responsibility. They make the oil and gas industry look far worse than it really is."

"I think it's far worse than anyone thinks it is," Lucy says.

We are becoming too loud and I can see other patrons turning around, so I think it best to change the subject.

"Well, it's only hypothetical, guys," I say. "No one's going to hack into any computers. I have enough trouble forwarding an email."

"That's not true, Tanzie. I thought . . ." I glare at my sister and she stops mid-sentence.

Thankfully, our entrées arrive, and Lucy shifts the conversation to her latest endeavors. To the relief of the other diners, we are now much quieter. Kim seems to have forgotten all about Lucy's suggestion that she cleanse her inherited guilt by divesting herself of all her oil-and-gas-gotten possessions. She is delightedly listening to Lucy's latest stories about shooting coyotes with paintball guns and making chickens lay multicolored eggs. This is Lucy's engaging, charming side, and I enjoy the respite from the Bishop conversation.

"So were you named after Lucille Ball?" Kim asks as our food consumption wanes.

"Actually, yes. I look like a Lucy," Lucy says laughing.

"Lucy is number seven in the family and I am number eight," I say. "Our parents let the older kids name the babies when they came home. It was sort of a way to ease jealousy and make it fun."

"Like a pet?"

"Sort of," I allow. "Anyway, when Lucy came home in July 1956 and had a head of red hair, the only one in the family, the kids all voted to name her Lucy."

"Thank goodness I wasn't a boy!" Lucy laughs. "I'd probably be called Howdy."

"So where did Tanzie come from?" Dan asks.

"Well, when Tanzie came home," Lucy begins, "we were watching *You Bet Your Life*—you know, that game show with Groucho Marx? He had two sisters on, Tanzie and Dorcas, who won all the money. When we voted, Tanzie beat out Dorcas by my single vote."

"Yes, barely a toddler and she got the swing vote determining my future," I say.

"I might have had some help." Lucy laughs.

"Wow, I've never heard of anything like that before." Kim looks at Dan.

"We have a fairly unique family," I say.

"Oh yes." Lucy laughs. "That we do."

We spend the rest of the evening retelling classic O'Leary family stories, from the litany of unusual houseguests to the menagerie of pets that also took advantage of our open-door policy. "In those days no one had leashes or anything. You fed the dog. The dog stayed around, so it was your dog," Lucy says.

"Alexander was this huge standard poodle mix with a mass of gray curls. We'd had him all of a week when he bit the mailman three times, so animal control showed up at the door and took Alexander away and issued my father a ticket. He was furious. 'I feed a stray dog and now it's my problem? I need to go to court? Ridiculous!'" Lucy has the brogue down perfectly.

"So we all go to court and my father tells the judge, 'Everyone else is eating off the government, why shouldn't my dog?'"

Kim and Dan howl with laughter. "Your father sounds like a real character," Kim says.

"Both our parents were," Lucy responds. "They've been gone for quite a while, though."

"So, did you ever get another dog?" Dan asks.

"We never saw poor Alexander again," I answer. "But we had another stray take up residence by the weekend. We never turned anyone away."

CHAPTER FIFTEEN

Against my suggestion, we decide to forgo dessert and instead walk back to the condos, saying our good-byes in the hall.

"So what was that at dinner, Lucy?" I ask as I take my coat off. "Did you talk to Dan about what we're doing?"

"No. I told you I didn't," Lucy says defensively.

"You never answered my question before," I correct. "You sure hinted around that you did."

"I was just playing with you, Tanzie. Lighten up."

I see no useful purpose in continuing along these lines and elect to change the subject.

"So what did you find today?" I ask as I watch Lucy divide what remains of the zinfandel between our glasses.

"Quite a bit, actually. These guys are real bastards. They have all kinds of environmental issues. They pay the fines when they are caught, but they do nothing to take preventive action. They have a gas plant near Longview, Texas, that is spewing CO, NOX, VOCs, formaldehydes, and H_2S, way over regulatory limits. From the files, it looks like they fudge on their reporting. I don't know why the TCEQ hasn't shut them down; I would think they would be fairly visible."

"You've lost me, Lucy."

"In layman's terms, there are limits on what can be released into the air. The company is supposed to measure emissions and report them to the regulatory agency, in this case the Texas Council for Environmental Quality, or TCEQ. Those poor people who live out there are breathing really bad air and don't know it. The plant dates back to the '60s, and I can't figure out why the TCEQ hasn't been on their doorstep doing their own independent testing.

"There is a reference to an entity called BQR Environmental Services, but I don't know what Bishop uses them for. There are a couple of memos indicating that they rely on this service to mitigate the damages. I don't see how, though. The internal plant measurements show very high levels that are completely different on the regulatory reports they send in. I think we have enough to at least call the enforcement division and file a complaint."

"BQR Environmental Services," I repeat. "Let me do some research on it first, okay, Lucy?"

"Why?" she asks, suddenly upset. "Why do you always take their side?"

"I'm not taking sides, Lucy. I'm just being prudent. It's a good thing. I don't jump to conclusions. I don't alert the media. I don't shout from the rooftops!"

"You don't do anything!" Lucy accuses. "You're so worried

about your reputation among those debutantes you hang out with in Houston. 'Oh my goodness. Maybe they won't invite me to the gala or something.' Why can't you see past your silly little life? Why don't you want something with more meaning?"

"Like sitting in a jail cell? That kind of meaning?" I ask, furious. "I don't expect you to want what I want, but you need to know that I *am* on your side here. We agree on a lot of things, Lucy. I just want to take time to pull it all together. If you release information too early, people have time to spin it their way. You know how to read environmental records, but I know how to investigate things. That's what I do. So let me investigate my way."

Lucy looks at me, and I can tell the wheels are spinning under that mop of red curls.

"Okay," she says finally. "But you have one week to take action on this Longview plant. There are real people who will get sick, and I am not comfortable sitting on that knowledge without taking action. The pipeline thing you can figure out on your own, or call me if you need more help. But I'm not like you, Tanzie. I feel too deeply for people."

Point taken once again, Lucy. "All right. Fair enough." I am instantly relieved I had not burdened Lucy with the meeting notes about the Bishop cover-up. I can see now that would have been a disaster.

"So what about the meeting? What did you hear?" Lucy pumps as she drains the rest of her wine.

"Not too much. Just posturing. Insurance stuff. Nothing too conclusive," I lie.

———◆———

When I get to my cube the next morning, I have two things I want to investigate: Do hot flashes burn calories, and who is BQR Environmental Services?

If hot flashes in fact do burn calories, then perhaps there is an upside to the discomfort I have been feeling lately and I will be wearing smaller pants soon. Google has conflicting answers and nothing scientifically compelling, so I move on to the second item. There is nothing on Google regarding BQR. So I look at the payment register, noting what looks like a monthly $5,000 payment to them dating back as far as the report goes. I write down the check number for one of the payments and take the elevator up to Corporate Accounting on twenty. I have been here a few times before while doing walk-throughs for my audits.

I see Cindy in the file room and ask if she can pull a canceled check for me.

"Check 260112 from the general account."

"We don't get the checks," she explains, "but we get copies from the bank statements."

"Does it have the back side, so I can see the endorsement?"

"No. But I can request it from the bank. Do you want me to?"

"How long will it take?"

"Not sure. Maybe I can get online and see if I can access it without bothering them."

"Thanks, Cindy. I appreciate it."

Cindy is one of the most efficient people at Bishop. She is a tad grumpy and her dress is so flashy that it borders on clownish. Her permed platinum hair is festooned with sequined combs, and she favors costume jewelry in the form of huge earrings, numerous bangles, and a ring larger than most plumbing fixtures. Cindy's bowling-alley style notwithstanding, she is usually invaluable for getting information quickly and accurately. In the time it takes me to check out the coffee bar and get a glass of ice water to cool down the inferno blazing from my neck, Cindy has gotten what I need.

"Here you go, Tanzie," she says, proudly handing me the documents.

I take the check copy and look at the endorsement, noting the first of many red flags. There is no stamp "For Deposit Only," used by most companies to restrictively endorse the checks they receive. Instead, the check has a name signed on the back. I can't decipher the signature. Only the *Q* between the first and last names is legible. I take the check copy with me back to my desk on six and ponder what to do.

I decide to go to the TCEQ website, and there is, of all things, an organization chart going all the way from the governor of Texas and other elected officials to the field-level flunkies responsible for doing the inspections. The letter *Q* stands out as the middle initial of Bonnie Q. Reynolds, a field inspector in the north Texas region for air quality. Now this makes perfect sense. Bonnie is looking the other way on the Longview plant and taking a nice payment for the effort. I wonder how many other inspectors are on the take. I also wonder if similar arrangements have been made with the DOT for the Houston pipeline. *Why hasn't the Department of Transportation done their inspections? No one said anything at the meeting the other night.* I am deep in thought and speculation when Todd stops by my cube.

"What's up?" I ask, shoving my paperwork into my desk drawer.

"It's Wednesday. Don't tell me you forgot. Coffee Wednesday. You weren't here last week."

"Oops. Sorry, Todd. I was . . . um, sick . . . well, out of town, but don't tell anybody." I smile sheepishly. I grab my purse and we head to the elevators.

"That new coffee in the break room is horrible," Todd says as we wait. "Did you know they changed from Starbucks?"

"Yeah, I think I read it somewhere."

We walk over to a trendy little place adjacent to the Bishop building that I can only assume will triple its revenue given the switch to Best Java at Bishop. I pay for Todd's coffee and my latte and walk over to a booth near the front window.

"Wanna hear something funny?" Todd begins. "Baldwin called the Help Desk Monday because he needed to change his password. He didn't know how to do it unless it was about to expire and gave him a prompt. He needed me to walk him through it. Here he runs this huge company and can't figure out how to change his password."

My shaking hand starts to make little waves in my latte.

"Why did he need it changed?" I ask trying not to act too interested.

"Well, actually he thinks his computer got hacked," Todd whispers, leaning toward me.

"Really."

"What I heard is that he tried to log in to his computer over the weekend but it was locked. The error notice said he was the user locking it. Then when he was able to log in, the screen was in some confidential file or something. I'm not sure, but he was pretty hot about it. There's some forensic specialist coming up here from Dallas next week. I have to get a workspace set up for him down on our floor."

"What will he be able to do?"

"Well, he can create a list of the IP addresses accessing Baldwin's account and then see where they are coming from."

"Oh really. How can they tell where the IP address comes from?" I ask, trying not to spill my latte as I bring it to my mouth.

"Well, they can only get within a geographic range, like Moscow or New York. In order to find out who owns the IP address, it usually takes a court order, and that could take over a year."

I relax a bit as I take in that last factoid. "Sounds complicated."

I look at my watch. "We need to head back, Todd. I'm sort of in the middle of something."

"Sure. No problem." Todd and I get up and head back to the Bishop building.

"Thanks for the coffee, Tanzie," Todd says as the elevator door opens on the third floor.

"You're very welcome, Todd. Very welcome."

———————◆———————

I sit at my desk and try to process this new information. I make a mental list of all the places from which I have hacked into Baldwin's computer. There is the Internet café in Houston, but I used cash. There is the library, but surely the librarian won't remember me. Even if she does, the description of a dumpy middle-aged woman with expensive shoes will hardly be incriminating. Then I remember my initial login from Grant's computer. That could be a problem. Still, if Todd is right, Baldwin and his investigator will not have that information, so I needn't take immediate action. I calm down and focus on the positives. At least I know what is going on, so I have that in my favor.

I am not finished investigating the payment to Ms. Bonnie Q.

Reynolds yet, so I go up to nine and park myself by good old Mazie's desk.

"Hi, Mazie. Do you remember me?" I ask.

"Why, of course I do," she says. "What brings you to my part of the woods?"

"I am looking for the vendor setup form for a vendor named BQR Environmental Services. It's probably a few years back, but I am wondering if you could pull it for me."

"Why do you need to see that?"

"I'm in Internal Audit, didn't I say?"

I see the blood drain from Mazie's face.

"Anyway I'm doing a test of vendor setup records," I say. "I requested a bunch of them last week from your supervisor, but this is an extra item that needs to be pulled."

I watch as Mazie tries to stay calm. I cannot imagine the stress she is feeling at this particular moment, with the realization that auditors are looking at vendor setup.

"Well now. Just give me a minute here to look this up," she says, and I watch her trembling hand click through a few screens on her desktop. "Looks like we set their record up in 2003. I'm not sure we still have those files on-site; they may be in storage somewhere."

"Can you check, please?" This is not Cindy I'm dealing with.

I can see that Mazie wants me gone and is probably thinking maybe the fastest way is to find the document, give it to me, and hope that I will not return to stumble across her illicit activity. *Too late, Mazie.* But still, she returns in minutes with a document.

"Do you need a copy, or do you just want to take a look at this?"

"I just need to look at it."

Mazie hands me the paper. I turn it over and look at the approval signature.

"Hal!" I do not believe my eyes at first, but when I consider it, this does make sense. Hal had overseen all those operations back then. Still, I cannot picture Hal—the great guy Hal, the father figure Hal—involved in a bribery scheme. He is the person who approved the setup of BQR. There are no other authorizations on the page. I suppose if I pull the monthly invoices, I will see his signature on them too.

"Mazie, would you mind if I make a quick copy of this?"

"Help yourself." She seems relieved that I am not asking for anything related to MCAL Electric or Larson Consulting.

When I return to my cube, I call Lucy on her cell. Her voice sounds like I just woke her up.

"Meet me for coffee?"

"Where, when?" she groans.

"Starbucks Utica Square, in fifteen minutes."

CHAPTER SIXTEEN

Lucy looks as beautiful as always. For a fifty-three-year-old woman who just rolled out of bed, that is something of an accomplishment. She is reading a book and drinking herbal tea, so I place my coffee order without disturbing her.

"Let's move outside so we won't be overheard," I say.

We settle under an arbor away from other patrons.

"And you're surprised by this?" Lucy asks after I tell her about Hal.

"Yes! Why shouldn't I be? He is a sexist and condescending, but I never did think he was a crook."

"Did it ever occur to you that the entire management of Bishop is crooked? Baldwin certainly knows what Hal did because it was in his secretary's files, right? This is no secret."

Lucy is right about this, and it occurs to me that corruption extends deep into the Bishop organization. In controls talk it's known as "tone at the top." This means that if the most senior executives cheat, others below will see that behavior as acceptable and will cheat as well. It works the other way around, too. If executive management sets the tone that cheating or skirting the rules will not be tolerated, others below them fall in line. The trouble is that executives always say that they expect everyone to operate with integrity, but then they wink when the top sales guy takes a kickback or their big deal maker spends thousands in strip clubs.

Sometimes the higher-ups give the message to work within the company guidelines of honesty, excellence, stewardship, and all the other "who we are" statements, but then supervisors place extreme pressure on line management to make their quotas. "Rank and yank" is the term used at evaluation time to forcibly rank all employees and then fire the bottom-feeders who, for whatever reason, have fallen short. No excuses, just results.

At Bishop, management receives their annual bonus based on earnings and nothing else. Winston used to say, "You get what you pay for." So if all you care about is the bottom line, people will do everything they can to increase that figure, even if it crosses into unethical territory. It might start innocently enough, but it can quickly end up in shifty accounting and side-stepping costly regulatory requirements.

Top management gets to be top management because they are competitive people who want to be winners. They might gamble with their employees' safety as well as the safety of communities so that they don't end up as the guy with the shitty quarterly earnings and miss their bonus targets. The poor fellow who says, "Well, we didn't make any money, but everyone is safe, and we are beloved by the community in which we operate" gets zilch and a quick boot to the curb.

Perhaps not all Bishop main managers are crooks, but the environment is perfect for managers to slide into the world of bribes, kickbacks, and manipulated financial results.

I think about Hal and the pressure he must have been under to succumb to illegal activity. I wonder what the conversation with the Bishop brothers was like when they discussed what to do about the Longview plant. The thing was old and held together with the engineering equivalent of duct tape. Necessary repairs would have been costly, and Hal would never have been able to meet his financial targets if fines were levied.

Maybe Hal set up this bribe and then got his promotion to oversee all the gas plant operations. Perhaps the Bishops appreciated his resourcefulness in saving all the capital maintenance dollars required to get the Longview plant up to spec by bribing the state inspector. He probably got rewarded with extra bonus money for going the extra mile. A new house for Nancy and Disney World vacations with the kids probably soothed whatever gremlins ate at his conscience.

The pressure to succeed can be formidable for men like Hal. They have been winners all their lives, and the idea that their career might get sidetracked can be devastating. No wonder he seemed despondent when he left the other day. He had played the game and then got sacked two yards from the goal line.

"Lucy, these things are more complicated than you think," I say. "Morality is not black and white—it has lots and lots of gray."

"Oh really. And exactly what shade of gray is bribing government regulators to look the other way when you spew carcinogens into the breathing space of unsuspecting citizens?"

"I'm not talking about the end result. I'm talking about how people—you know, the ones you feel so deeply for—find themselves able to commit unthinkable acts. It can be a very slippery slope."

"No it's not."

"Yes it is. They don't start out wanting to break laws and hurt people. They just find themselves backed against a wall and make really bad decisions. It's really sad, Lucy."

"I don't feel sorry for them. Not even a little bit. I feel sorry for the people who live in Longview who are getting sick while you're sympathizing with the guys responsible."

"Okay. You're right," I concede. I take a sip of my coffee and look around; we are still alone. "We need to figure out what to do about this."

"I am serious about the one-week deadline, Tanzie," Lucy says. "I'm not comfortable sitting on this, especially since we now know that Bishop bribed the regulators."

"Agreed."

"Maybe you should call Dan and arrange to be a confidential informant."

The same thought had crossed my mind on the way to Starbucks, but I feel conflicted. There is a slim chance that I could keep my job at Bishop, and I don't want to take a chance of screwing that up by having anyone know that I snooped around Bishop's files. I am also smart enough to realize that confidences can be broken through negligence: slip of the tongue, a discarded memo. A further complication is the cyber investigator that Todd told me about yesterday. I am unclear what techniques this guy might have at his disposal to identify me as the hacker, and as compelling as the Longview situation is, I am not willing to risk getting caught. Yes, I am a very self-ish person.

"I think I like the anonymous informant idea better. If we provide enough detail, surely someone can get Hal or Ms. Bonnie Q. Reynolds to admit guilt, or we can give enough details to get an investigation going."

We go back to my condo and spend the rest of the morning documenting the Longview plant situation. Lucy writes a memo in environmental science-ese outlining the discrepancies between internal plant measurement and compliance reports filed with the TCEQ. I decide to spare Lucy from knowing about Baldwin's discovery that his computer was hacked and his engaging a security specialist. I only warn her not to communicate with me via email on any of the particulars of Longview or Bishop.

She has a flight to catch at 1 o'clock, so she packs up and we get in my car to head to the airport.

"We're doing the right thing on this, Tanzie. Really we are," Lucy begins as I drive.

"I know," I say, looking ahead.

"I didn't mean those things I said last night about your life being silly."

"Yes you did," I tell her. "And it is sort of silly. I know that. But I'm just trying to get my life back, Lucy. It's been a tough year for me."

We are silent for the next few miles. I am trying not to cry, and Lucy gives me time to compose myself.

"This has been so much fun," I finally say, just as the floodgates open.

Lucy doubles over in a combination of laughter and tears. "Oh God. Don't make me feel bad!"

"No. I really needed you here, Lucy. We don't always agree, but I really did need someone to work through this with me. I feel very alone on this, and you've been a lot of help."

"Thanks. I know I can be a fanatic sometimes."

"Sometimes?" I pull up curbside to the United Airlines drop-off and give my sister an awkward hug as she adjusts her backpack in the passenger seat.

"Let me know what happens," she says as she gets out of my car. "I love you."

"Me, too," I shout out the window as I watch my sister push through the glass doors to the ticketing terminal.

———◆———

I go back to the office to use my computer to establish an electronic document trail that could be given to even the least capable government auditor for follow-up. It takes awhile to put a paper trail of reports together, but around six or so, I am satisfied with my product.

As I stand at the post office dropbox, I take a deep breath, thinking about what I am about to do. Up until this point, it has just been a lot of talking. Once I mail the files, it will be real. People will know about Bishop. People will speculate as to how all this was discovered. I know how these things play out. Who has access to the files? Who has an axe to grind? I am sure that I have adequately covered my tracks, but what if everyone thinks Sullivan is the whistleblower? I could see the Bishops talking about "that nincompoop in EH&S" again and administering punishment on an innocent guy. Still, if I don't do this, Lucy will, and then it would be fairly easy to track me down. It would not take long to figure out that Lucy O'Leary, environmental Nazi, has a sister who works at Bishop.

Maybe if Sullivan had been a little nicer to the cleaning lady the decision would have been harder. But just as many others on the horns of dilemmas do, I elect to save my own patootie.

I pull open the slot for domestic first-class mail and slowly watch the legal envelopes drop out of my hand: the first to the enforcement division of the TCEQ, the second to the Oklahoma City district office of the FBI, and a third to the *Tulsa World* newspaper, attention Dan Schweitzer.

To celebrate my divorce from a life of silliness, I drive to Woodward Park, a lovely botanical garden near my condo, and sit on a bench near an expanse of azaleas just starting to bloom. I think about Sullivan and Hal and the people in Longview. I think about the Bishops. I think about the cyber security guy. It is getting dark as I watch the joggers and dog walkers go by, and I light a cigarette, exhaling into the crisp Tulsa air.

———◆———

The next Monday, I call in to the executive meeting and chuckle silently when Baldwin discloses that he has received a call from a *Tulsa World* reporter asking for a comment on bribery allegations involving Bishop and the TCEQ.

"Judas Priest! That has absolutely no foundation, none at all," he fumes. "But of course I told him we simply do not comment on unfounded rumors."

Oh, just you wait, I think. *Wait until the FBI shows up at the door.*

The Project Titanic update includes the revelation that there will be a 20 percent reduction in force this Friday.

"Many shared service teams will be outsourced, including Accounts Payable, Payroll Processing, and IT," Skip reports.

Poor Todd, I think. Even worse, I'd forgotten all about the cupcakes I'd promised him.

But just then, I lost my ability to worry too much about other people's employment: "Internal Audit, Community Relations, and Employee Training will be eliminated altogether."

What? So the fraud discovery hasn't saved us? I gave the write-up to Frank on Friday, as asked, but haven't heard anything. It is really too early in the morning for Frank to have met with Jim, so maybe there could be a reprieve once Jim and Skip have a chance to reevaluate things.

"Thanks for that update, Skip," Bennet adds, and with that I hear the three phone chimes indicating Skip has hung up from the conference. Immediately after he is gone, Bennet continues, "I'll be sorry to see Skip go."

"It can't be helped, Bennet." This is from Baldwin. "We just can't do what we have to do as well as Farley Solutions. Really a stroke of genius finding them."

Farley is a huge HR outsourcing firm in Dallas. Winston used their Houston branch over the years. So that means all of HR is going; probably not on Friday, but sometime shortly after that. Most likely right after they have put in their all-nighters to prepare for this mass layoff.

Damn! The only person with any stroke at Bishop who understands my capabilities is a short timer. I scowl at the receiver.

The meeting continues, taking longer than usual because of all the updates on the Houston explosion. The situation does not look good for Bishop, and preliminary results indicate that terrorism was not a factor. Damage by construction or sewer crews has been deemed unlikely, but has not yet been ruled out completely by the investigation team in Houston. Legal reports that outside counsel will be filing certain preemptive motions later today and that only small progress has been made on getting injured parties to accept settlement payments.

Things break up by 9:30, and after I hang up I surf through my documents file to begin the depressing task of updating my resume. There isn't much to add for my six months at Bishop, and the idea of doing this all over again for some other company sends my stomach churning.

I get on some job websites. There isn't anything in Tulsa and very little in Houston. Most companies want at least a supervisor-level auditor. The job market is still struggling nationwide.

I jump like a nervous cat when Frank sneaks up behind me, coffee cup in hand, asking me to come into his office. "Pull the door closed, please," he says as I enter. Has he somehow figured out I have been eavesdropping on the executive meeting? Has the cyber security guy contacted him? I bite my lower lip, waiting to hear what he has to say.

"I just met with Jim and Skip about the fraud in Accounts Payable," Frank begins.

"What did they think of the write-up?" I am trying not to give away that I have just heard our department is being eliminated. I wonder if Frank has been able to impact the plan I've heard about at the meeting. "Are we going to prosecute?"

"No." I detect a little shame and frustration in Frank's tone. "Jim took this all the way up the chain, while I was in his office. Bishop does not want to chance any publicity indicating that they are mismanaged in any way. They have decided just to let the employees go."

"Frank, you saw how much they stole—it's in the millions. Of course, it is confusing and I can't be sure," I add out of sheer habit.

"Even more reason to keep it quiet." I can tell this rankles Frank. There is nothing worse for an auditor than to uncover a fraud and have management look the other way. There will be no framed handshake photo ops for Frank. No assholes sitting in jail. "They need you to put together a list of the payments."

"Why do they want that?" I ask.

"They just want to write off the payments in the accounts."

I blink. "So these women get off scot-free?"

"'Fraid so. Look, I don't like this any more than you do."

"Are they going to at least remove their system access?" I ask. "When are they going to fire them?"

"Friday. I think."

Same as the rest of us.

"So these women just keep on stealing until Friday and they don't even get anything in their personnel files about this?"

"Tanzie, it's not my decision."

"Well, Frank," I say, getting a little loud, "it is just so like Bishop to dump their garbage on everyone else's front lawn. If they don't file charges, these gals will move on to the next employer and do the same thing."

"Tanzie, I agree with you, but there is nothing I can do about it. The decision has been made already. Let's just get Jim what he needs and move on."

We will be moving on, all right. All of us.

"When do you need this by?" I ask.

"Jim would like it by the end of the week. Friday, first thing?"

"Sure. No problem." My face is red, perhaps from a hot flash, or more likely from the anger of letting Mazie off the hook and me looking at unemployment. And there is a horrible irony in all of this: Mazie and Amy *and I* will get exactly the same recommendation from Bishop. They will land on their feet, but I won't. It doesn't matter that Skip knows I am the brains behind the fraud discovery. No one cares. The unfairness of all this is galling.

"One more thing, Tanzie," Frank says. "I checked back on the audit I did last year at Boyd, and our scope did not include a review of vendor setup. I wanted you to know that."

At lunch I drive down to the library again to take a look at Baldwin's e-mail and calendar that I accessed through Marla's account. I notice that on Friday from 10:00 to 10:30 he is scheduled for "Titanic," which means he will be speaking to the lucky 80 percent who get to keep their jobs. I remember that Winston, in a similar circumstance, had to tell his staff that as sad as it was to watch coworkers leave, the remaining work-force should feel complimented that they were so valuable. They were the winners.

Actually, they are not necessarily winners. Yes, they will keep their jobs and are spared the humiliation of having to tell their friends and neighbors that they were let go. They will not have to make those embarrassing phone calls to professional col-leagues "touching base," "testing the waters," or arranging for networking lunches. They will not have to suffer the awkward-ness of unreturned messages and the standard "I'll let you know if I hear anything" from the employed population.

The survivors, though, are left inside a company full of belt tightening: no Christmas party, lousy bonuses, and the elimination of all Styrofoam cups and plastic cutlery. Health insurance premiums will increase, and there will be no raises. Meanwhile, private planes and off-site management boondoggles will continue for the executive team, as well as deferred compensation plans for which the proletariat does not qualify. I know all the tricks well, since I have been an indirect beneficiary of big-ass executive compensation programs.

I am now on the other end. I am only entitled to two-weeks' pay and a swift kick in the rear. There will be no corner office for Tanzie Lewis. My career, despite my best efforts, is done. My six months in the workforce has resulted in a layoff, which is code to all future employers for "you weren't valuable enough to keep around."

I return to the office after lunch and wander down to the third floor in search of Todd. I have once again forgotten about the cupcakes but I really want to meet the cyber security specialist and try to find out exactly what he will be doing. Todd escorts me to a small office near the server room.

"Tanzie Lewis, Internal Audit." I extend my hand.

"Raj Basu," he says, standing up and smiling. Raj is tall, dark, and round with a thick head of black hair. He looks about forty years old, but I can't be sure. He is one of those guys who don't get wrinkles, lose their hair, or go gray.

"I'm not an IT specialist, but I do most of the IT-related audits, so if there's anything I can help you with, just let me know," I say.

"I don't think that will be necessary," Raj says coldly. "But thanks for the offer." He sits back down and faces his computer screen, signaling the conversation is over.

Raj is all business and is not to be charmed into discussing the investigation. Still, I now know what he looks like and where his office is, so it isn't a total waste of time.

"He's a lot of fun," I say to Todd as we walk to the elevator.

"You were expecting what? This is IT, remember."

"You're an IT guy, and you're fun, Todd," I say. "Keep me posted if you hear anything. I think this hacking thing is pretty interesting, don't you?"

"Okay, Tanzie. Will do. You already owe me cupcakes from two weeks ago, you know."

I leave the third floor with an uneasy feeling in my gut. I again sit at my desk thinking about what Raj will find out. As far as I can tell, my only slip was accessing Baldwin's account from Grant's computer. But that was just for a second or two, and I never got beyond the login screen. Maybe that will be chalked up to some cyber anomaly and not followed up. It horrifies me to think that I may be exposed as the hacker, the informant, the saboteur. Perhaps I can provide a red herring for Raj. I know from experience that evidence that is tied up with a bow for someone to find can eclipse some of the more subtle things that take time and money to figure out. If I can provide something to make Raj's investigation quick and easy, perhaps he will blow off getting a court order to identify my initial login from the McAfees'.

Unfortunately, I have no immediate ideas about what evidence I can manufacture, but I am satisfied momentarily and begin to relax.

CHAPTER SEVENTEEN

When I get home just before five o'clock I feel beat. I pour a glass of wine and flip on the news as I cuddle up on my couch. The local news comes on with a lead reporter stationed in front of the Bishop building. According to her story, the Bishop Group has earlier today filed documents claiming that "third-party negligence" is responsible for the explosion. Allegedly a sewer contractor weakened the pipe with some work done in 2009, and the victims of the blast—fifty-seven dead, scores injured, and a neighborhood destroyed—could be considered guilty of contributory negligence. So this is the legal move I heard about in this morning's meeting.

No further elaboration is given on the story, and even the national news has nothing other than what got reported locally. A Bishop spokesman indicates that the filing is part of a larger complaint and that it is standard in matters such as these. They are not blaming the victims per se, just making some preemptive legal moves that are considered prudent under the circumstances.

Don't you worry, I think. *Just sit tight and wait for the Bishop boys to hang themselves with this.*

I go out on my balcony for my customary evening smoke and to take stock of my situation. My successful husband dumped his old and lumpy wife for a beautiful, young, successful woman. My share of our accumulated wealth took a serious dive in the economic crisis, and with this layoff, any hope I may have had of resurrecting my career is over. I have a cyber security specialist on my tail who can create all kinds of legal problems for me down the road. Still, yesterday, I got to use my skills on behalf of the people of Longview, Texas, and that is just about the only thing that makes this otherwise horrible day more palatable.

Maybe Lucy is right. Maybe if I think less about myself and more about humanity things will improve overall. I am never going to get my old life back, never have a real career, but maybe I can have something even better and all my own.

I sublet this condo from an oil company employee stationed in Russia until August, so only the linens and towels actually belong to me. I can fit everything, including my golf clubs, in the trunk of my Lexus and hit the road anytime I want to. I can pack up and leave at a moment's notice, and except for the remaining rent payments on the condo, I never even have to think about Tulsa again. All I have to do is pick the right moment to go. I have only a few days of employment left at Bishop, and I start thinking about what I can accomplish during that time frame.

———◆———

There is no one left on the executive floor this Tuesday evening as I take a moment to survey the territory and sit at Marla's desk. There is a security camera, but it is pointed toward the elevators. While security might see a cleaning lady get off on the floor, they will not be able to see me at Marla's desk or in Baldwin's office now or later if they decide to pull the tapes.

My hands are shaking as I log in using MWALTERS on Marla's computer and upload LEAR_2008_17_Houston_Gas into her file. I save a backup copy in the 2005 folder and leave a hard copy among some other paperwork she keeps in the one unlocked file cabinet drawer I found previously. I also upload the recorded meeting from the other night onto Marla's machine, stored in a file labeled Misc. If the Department of Justice does a sweep, surely they will find these files. I look under Marla's pen set and almost fall over laughing. Baldwin's new password is recorded there, right next to the old one. GOJayhawks!18—he only changed one digit in response to a security breach. Why am I surprised? This is unexpected, and I can't help myself as I look around the abandoned floor. With Raj on my tail, accessing Baldwin's computer remotely will leave a trail, but it certainly won't if I use his desktop. I smile at the many possibilities circulating in my brain as I sit in Baldwin's enormous leather chair.

In less than five minutes, I reconfigure his date/time function to a week ago. I quickly compose the following e-mail:

SULLIVAN,
PLEASE TAKE A MOMENT TO REVIEW THE FILES
WITH RESPECT TO RECENT EVENTS AND SANITIZE

THEM ACCORDINGLY. I DO NOT WANT ANYTHING
REGARDING THE HOUSTON PIPELINE BLOW-UP TO
REMAIN IN ANY OF OUR FILES.
REGARDS,
BRB

Send. Done. When the "could not deliver" notification
chimes because of the slight difference in Sullivan's address, I
quickly delete it. If Baldwin checks his iPhone, there will be no
trace of this correspondence. I print out a hard copy and slide
it behind his credenza. The same investigators who will find the
files I left in Marla's office and on her computer will certainly
find this smoking gun.

I change back the date on the computer and re-sort his sent
file. The e-mail is there, but Baldwin would never think to look
in his sent file from a week ago. I compose a couple new e-mails,
deleting all of them from the sent file almost immediately after
they are sent. One brings me great joy: I email Rosie Daugherty,
the Accounts Payable Director, asking her to make some sizable
donations to Planned Parenthood, the Urban League, and the
Sierra Club. I finish up that e-mail with:

PLEASE DO NOT DISCUSS OR CORRESPOND WITH
ME IN THE FUTURE REGARDING THIS. I CANNOT
EXPLAIN THE PARTICULARS OF THIS REQUEST
RIGHT NOW, BUT YOUR DISCRETION ON THIS SEN-
SITIVE MATTER IS GREATLY APPRECIATED AND
WILL BE REWARDED VERY SOON.
ALL THE BEST,
BRB

I would give anything to know what the donation chairs of those charities will think when they open their envelopes containing $250K from the Bishop Group.

I take a moment to read today's e-mail but get interrupted when I hear the elevator chime. In my panic, I cannot remember if Baldwin's computer was completely turned off or only logged off when I arrived. I decide just to shut the computer down and get the hell out. I hear voices coming my way and take a deep breath. I am in Marla's office dusting when Baldwin and another man enter her vestibule.

"Where's Gloria?" Baldwin asks in a friendly tone.

"No English, señor," I reply, keeping my head down, focused on getting every inch of Marla's desk lamp cleaned.

"Must be new," I hear Baldwin say to the other pear-shaped man as they go into his office and shut the door.

I am shaking by the time I make it to the elevator but thrilled just the same. I am good at this, and it is a blast.

For my next task, I change elevator banks and take the car up to the eighth floor where the rank-and-file HR folks work. This is a dangerous move, but if I can pull it off, it will be well worth it. The elevator opens onto steadily humming and clicking office activity and plenty of movement by employees walking in and out of offices and leaning in doorways to ask questions. I am surprised at the activity but then remember how busy the HR folks are getting ready for Friday. *Abort* is my immediate inclination. This is way too dangerous an environment in which to implement my new plan, so instead of getting out, I remain in the elevator and ride down to the lobby.

Driving home, I realize that this has become sort of an addiction for me. The thrill becomes greater each time I am able to get away with my clandestine activity. It began on Easter Sunday, and it increased with hacking into Baldwin's files, then spying on Mazie, breaking in the other night, and then again this evening. I love it. It is better than sinking a killer putt to win a championship. I do not want it to end, ever.

And with what I am now planning, it will never have to.

CHAPTER EIGHTEEN

I am pretty sure that no one other than department heads, HR, and I know that the Project Titanic layoffs are scheduled for tomorrow. Common practice among large companies is not to fire people on a Friday, since they have the whole weekend to sulk and are unable to take any proactive measures in their job search until the following Monday. The hopelessness can result in depression, spousal abuse, and even suicide. Once again, Bishop is behind the curve of best practices.

The prevailing rumor is that the layoffs are scheduled for next Wednesday. Moe and Frank spend most of their days visiting with each other like a couple of old hens, speculating about organization changes. Other managers on the floor visit them, and then they all disappear together for hours on end. No work will get done until the axe falls.

I take the opportunity to clear out what few personal items

I brought to the office: a mug, my Windows XP bible, and an extra cigarette lighter. Without a family, there are no framed pictures, finger paintings from children, or doodads that people bring to make their workplace more like home. My cube reflects how truly temporary Tulsa is for me.

It is only 9:00 a.m. If I think strategically and focus on a clean execution, I can get everything I am planning done by lunch. I can feel my excitement building once again; most likely it's pretty similar to any addict anticipating the next hit.

I open up Word, goof around with fonts and formats until I achieve the desired results. I make a quick checklist of what has to be done and the information I will need in order to do it. I cannot forget a single thing or I will be in big trouble. On this one, I can't hide behind the cover of an auditor just doing my work.

I wander down to IT and find Todd at his terminal, talking some bewildered employee through a password change. He looks up and gives me the "just a minute" gesture.

"What can I do for you?" he asks. "And are there cupcakes involved?"

"Actually, yes. I think I still owe you from two weeks ago." I laugh, producing a small white box sealed with a golden bee sticker. "I didn't make these, but they're probably better anyway."

"Beehives! That is a treat." Todd beams. Beehives is a tiny restaurant bakery near my condo that produces first-class treats. I didn't have time to bake with all my snooping and my sister visiting, so I picked up four cupcakes this morning before work.

I watch as Todd opens the box and gingerly selects a cake with his thumb and index finger.

"I didn't have breakfast. I'm starving," he says, biting into his treat. "Want one?"

"Oh, no thanks, Todd. These are all for you."

"I'm having dinner with my parents tonight. I'll save the rest for them," Todd says, wiping his hand on a paper towel salvaged from his desk drawer.

I wonder about Todd and what will happen for him after tomorrow. IT is usually in demand even during hard times, so I suspect Todd will find something else fairly quickly. I hope so.

"Now how can I help you?"

"I have been asked to do a count of the cell phones turned in by the executives terminated on Monday. Do you know who I should talk to?"

"Yeah, follow me."

He introduces me to Sophie, a just-out-of-college type who is in charge of phones, laptops, and other small hardware items. I tell Sophie who I am and that Internal Audit is doing an inventory to make sure that all the company cell phones have been turned in by the former executives.

"I will need a list of names and phone IDs," I explain. "And then I will need to actually see each of the phones." This really is bullshit, because any auditor would have come with her own list, but Sophie doesn't know that. I can tell she is nervous about an auditor making sure she's done her job correctly.

"The phones are kept in this closet over here," she says. Quickly, she prints out a schedule of fifteen or so names, and then she walks me over to a closet door and unlocks it.

She watches me as I look at the list and dig through the shelves, looking for the corresponding phone. "It's better if I work alone on this," I say in the most authoritative tone I can muster. "I will let you know the results when I am finished."

"Yes ma'am," Sophie says, and she leaves. I quickly look through the list, find Hal's phone, and put it in my pocket.

After about twenty minutes or so, I return to Sophie's desk.

"I found all but this one," I say, pointing to Hal's name.

"I was sure I had them all." Sophie looks upset.

"Maybe it's just misplaced," I say. "Please just follow up and let me know if you find it. It's not a big deal, Sophie. I won't write it in the report."

"Oh God. Thank you," she says. She is almost in tears when I leave her for the stairwell.

There are only a couple of bars of reception on Hal's phone and the battery is weak, but I have what I need.

"Bishop Group," the cheerful receptionist answers.

"I have planted bombs on three floors of your building," I tell her using a fake voice. "They are set to go off at exactly eleven o'clock today. Fuck your company and everything they stand for." I hang up.

I know what the protocol is on something like this, as I audited the very process earlier in the year. The receptionist is supposed to call 911 immediately, followed by Building Services. A floor-by-floor evacuation then commences, and each department meets at a predefined location a block away from the building. Floor wardens and safety marshals wearing lovely orange vests will have checklists to make sure that all employees are accounted for and follow up on the ones they can't find. I have about five minutes before the process starts.

"Frank," I say, poking my head in his office, "I'm going up to the twentieth floor to find some files."

"Okay." He doesn't even look up from his desk.

I take my things and go to the ninth floor. I use my janitorial keys to let myself into a locked supply closet and wait, putting on the orange vest I took from my neighbor's cube before she got to work.

The alarms sound. I am sure most employees think it is a drill. I can hear the sound of orderly footsteps headed to the stairwells, just as they had been prepped in the annual rehearsals supervised by the Tulsa Fire Department.

"Please go to the lobby exit and meet at the northwest corner of the garage," the warden repeats over and over.

It takes about five minutes for the ninth floor to get to the stairwell and begin the long march down to the street. When I hear the all clear from the safety warden, indicating that there is no one left on the floor, I emerge from my hiding place and go to Mazie's cube.

It is still logged on, and I access the vendor maintenance screen, where I change the Cayman account number that receives the payments for Larson Consulting to my own.

I move over to Amy's cube. Her automatic logoff has kicked in, so I use the parsley password I found last week to gain access. I enter my invoice data and note that the wire has been put in the final approval queue. I log off and drop my self-constructed pre-approved invoice into one of the baskets in a neighboring cube.

I quickly hurry to the stairwell and join the parade of employees, which has thinned to a trickle. The Tulsa bomb squad and K-9 unit pass by us on the other side, going up. Outfitted in my official vest, no one notices as I enter the eighth floor, where I'd had to abort my mission last night. With the floor empty of its perky occupants, I go immediately to the comp file room and locate the stack of rate change authorization forms, taking two, in case I make a mistake later on. I place the forms in a manila folder to keep them from getting creased and head down the stairs.

My last stop is on six. Frank's office. From there, I log in to Baldwin's computer and download six or seven folders onto Frank's hard drive. This access will show up on Raj's radar screen like a giant red flag, and he will probably figure that Frank is responsible for the hacking. Raj doesn't know that Frank isn't capable of something like that. There won't be any reason to get court orders for the other access attempts. Again I head to the stairwell, dumping my vest in an empty cube on the way. Then I go to the designated meeting spot and check in with the safety representative.

"We were getting worried about you," Frank says.

"I was up on the twentieth floor and the stairwell was packed, so I thought I'd wait and get some of the files I needed." I gesture to my manila folder. "This is a drill, right?"

Evacuating all employees from a thirty-story building is no easy task, and getting them back in isn't, either. Recognizing this, the Building Services Director sends a handwritten message to each group saying that all employees who are nonessential should feel free to take lunch early. As the poster child for nonessentialness, I take him up on his offer and head toward the garage.

As I exit the elevator on five, I see Amy and Mazie over by the red Mercedes smoking cigarettes. I think about joining them but do not, offering instead a perfunctory wave and smile as I walk by.

I get in my car and drive off. I refuse to think of myself as Mazie's kindred spirit. I am not; for one thing, I dress better and have better hair. For another, I'm in it for the excitement and revenge. I steal from crooks, which is very different from stealing from regular people. Mazie doesn't know what I know about the Bishop Group and how they operate.

My rationalizations continue along those lines as I drive over the Arkansas River and throw Hal's former company phone into the only deep spot for miles. If by some remote chance the bomb threat is traced, it will be Hal's problem. For all I know, his name showed up on the receptionist's phone when the call came in. No real risk for Hal, since it is clear to me that Bishop is not interested in any negative publicity at the moment.

I try not to think about the theft or Hal or anyone at Bishop. The best rationalization strategy is to forget about it completely. What's done is done. Move on.

I get back to my desk around one o'clock and bring up my Cayman account. My $500,000 wire had been received at exactly 12:15. I knew from my audits that wires are sent at 11:00 each morning, but because of the evacuation, today's had been delayed.

The other evening, when I had planned out exactly what I was going to do, I had run the cost projections for college tuition, not just for Lulu but for a scholarship fund in honor of my godson Matt. Returns on investments are grim at the moment, but if a significant corpus could be set up, it would be poised for the next bull market. It is only prudent investing.

I just about choke when I see that three more wires have also hit the account, each for $50,000. I guess these were ones Amy had already put in the queue herself. *Wow. An extra $150K. Thank you, Amy and Mazie.* I cancel the account online and move the balance into my account in Houston. There might be some taxes and paperwork involved, but it is free money, after all, so who cares? The unexpected windfall can be used for personal benefit.

One thing becomes clear as I sit in my cube, adjusting the waistband of my pants as they cut into my midsection flab. My appearance has reached a critical low point, and I have to do something. Being an accountant, I prepare a cost analysis and timeline to support what I think I will need for this new project: my transformation from Ernest Borgnine to maybe not Madonna, but something closer to that end of the spectrum. All in, I am looking at around $100K, which includes some cosmetic surgery and a few months at La Costa, shedding blubber and getting my golf game back.

There will also be enough to get me set up back in Houston with a membership at Ravenswood Country Club. I call the Atlanta plastic surgeon, and due to the poor economy, I am able to set up a consultation for early next week. I marvel at what I am able to accomplish. Not a bad morning's work.

Todd from IT supplies an updated list of disbursements, and I start on my compilation of Mazie and Amy's fraudulent transactions, making sure my wire is on the list to be written off, and I send it to Frank before packing up for the day.

Mahogany's Steakhouse is my next stop. I decide to celebrate my big day at the bar, alone, sipping a cucumber martini before savoring a spectacular lobster tail. The lobsters here are kept alive in a tank, so they're not as travel weary as the other seafood in Tulsa. As I sip my drink and look in the mirror behind the bar I notice someone with a familiar face walking up behind me.

"Hal! What are you doing here?"

"Double scotch on the rocks," Hal calls to the bartender by way of an answer.

"You drink? I thought you were a Southern Baptist?"

"It's a recent development." He talks loudly, the way people do when they're drunk, and I guess this isn't Hal's first bar of the evening. "Just don't ask me to go out dancing. Ha!" Hal swivels the stool next to mine and sits down.

"I heard you were let go. I'm so sorry, Hal."

"Fucking Bishops! Gave them my whole damn life and they throw me away like yesterday's newspaper." *Wow, vulgarity out of Hal too. I am definitely seeing a different side of my former boss.*

"I know what that's like." I give Hal a knowing smile and take a bite of the cucumber slice that garnishes my cocktail.

"You don't know any of it, Tanzie. Got a goddamn subpoena from the TCEQ this morning. My life is shit. What'll I tell Nancy?" Hal downs his scotch and waves for another.

"Slow down, Hal," I caution. "How are you getting home?"

"You don't know what it's like, Tanzie. Spent my whole life doing the right thing. Straight as an arrow. I make one mistake and I'm cooked."

"I've ordered dinner, Hal, do you want to move to a table?"

"This is my dinner." He holds up his fresh glass of scotch.

I take a long look at the man. *Lucy is wrong,* I think. *There's plenty of gray area sitting right here next to me.*

"Let me tell you something, Tanzie. You make one mistake. Just one. Cross over that line and your life is never the same." Hal downs the rest of his drink and signals the bartender for a check.

"I've got this, Hal," I say.

"Did you just win the lottery, Tanzie?" Hal smiles.

"Something like that." I smile back. "Just came into some family money."

"Well, thank you very much," Hal says and gets up from the barstool. Through the mirror I watch him stumble toward the door. The hostess guides Hal to a chair while she makes a phone call, presumably to a cab company. I think about giving Hal a ride home, but a waiter appears just then and sets my lobster tail down on the bar. My appetite is suddenly gone, and I flag the bartender.

"Can I get this to go? I'm sorry, I just can't stay."

"Certainly," he replies and takes my plate away. I pull my iPhone out of my purse and look up *Tulsa World*. I write Dan's name and work number on a cocktail napkin and walk over to Hal.

"I don't know what you've done, Hal," I lie. "But give this guy a call. He may be interested in what you have to say. You shouldn't have to be in this alone."

Hal grabs my hand as I put the folded the napkin into the breast pocket of his suit. "I always liked you, Tanzie. You're a sweetheart, girlie." He pats my hand as I pull it away.

"Thanks, Hal." I stop myself before I offer him a ride. What if he makes a pass at me or throws up in my Lexus? I decide not to take responsibility for Hal, even though I *am* more than a little bit responsible.

I walk back to the bar to collect the white plastic bag that contains my dinner. I take the last sip of my martini and think about what Hal said. I crossed a line today myself. But I didn't do it for greed, like Mazie and Amy. I didn't do it to get ahead in my career, like Hal. I did it to screw those "fucking Bishops" and add some excitement to my boring life. The plastic surgery fund was an unexpected bonus. Mine is a different line, I rationalize.

As I leave the steakhouse I pass Hal, who has fallen asleep in the chair by the exit. I give the hostess the to-go bag. "See that my friend over there takes this home with him."

"Of course," she replies.

Perhaps arriving home with a $90 lobster tail from Mahogany's will keep Nancy from tossing poor Hal out on his ear tonight.

Once home, I shower, wrap myself in my robe, and head out to the balcony for a smoke and telephone chat with Lucy.

"I was up all last night shooting at those damn coyotes," she says. "I'm not sure my strategy is working very well."

"Told ya." I laugh.

"Oh hey, I forgot. Bumby says that NYU wants the first tuition payment by the end of the month. Will you be able to take care of that?"

"Absolutely. And by the way, watch the news." I tell her about the *Tulsa World* inquiry from the meeting on Monday, but not about my misappropriation. Like my two cigarettes a day, that is my little secret.

CHAPTER NINETEEN

t is always interesting to see how companies handle mass layoffs. Employees generally watch the HR staff for the subtlest signals to fuel the rumor mill. Once, at a client's back in the day, I stumbled upon a whiteboard in a conference room that had been left and forgotten by the project team detailing a reduction in force. HR does not typically attract detail-oriented people. Perkiness seems to be the attribute most important for that career. But there will be no perkiness today at the Bishop Group.

A meeting notice is sent out to the entire corporate group at 12:01 a.m., indicating that an all-employee meeting is being held at the Hyatt down the street from our building at 10:00. Due to the large volume of attendees, employees are to observe meeting room assignments. One group will be in the main ballroom, and the "overflow" will watch on a closed-circuit TV in a smaller space. Employees assigned to the ancillary meeting room will be notified by a separate email. My separate email arrives shortly after the first, at 12:02 a.m. It is clear to me that there will be no closed-circuit feed, but rather tables of HR representatives who will process our severance while in the main ballroom Baldwin will deliver his congratulatory speech to the surviving members of the Bishop family.

People start leaving for the meeting around nine thirty; just as in the case of the bomb scare, it is hard for everyone to get out at the same time. Frank and Moe stop by my cube as they head to the crowded elevator bank.

"I'm taking the stairs," I tell them. "We're only on six, for heaven's sake." I grab my manila envelope and put it carefully into my purse before heading to the stairwell. I really need to start getting more exercise before my La Costa stay so I won't pass out during the morning hikes.

"Good idea," says Frank. "I'm in the little conference room, and I want to make sure I get a good seat."

I start to laugh as I follow the many others with the same idea, going down to street level, leaving the Bishop building for what maybe only I knew was the final time.

The mass of Bishop employees is funneling onto the Hyatt escalator up to the ballroom area. A sign at the top indicates that the main ballroom is to the left and the slaughterhouse is to the right. The herd parts at the top, and Frank, Moe, and I check in with a woman holding a clipboard at the entrance to the room. There are no HR processing desks set up, but there are no TVs, either. Moe and Frank become uneasy as they try to figure out how we will view the meeting. Our little room is filling up. I nod at Mazie and Amy, and they wave me over to sit next to them. Their boss, Rosie, is there, as are most employees in the Accounts Payable group.

"They're outsourcing us," I overhear Rosie whisper to the woman next to her. "They kept two of the managers to handle the transition, but they will be gone in three months." Amy and Mazie shift in their chairs when they hear this.

Cindy is there, and so are Sophie and Todd from IT. All in all, there are about one hundred employees, mostly older people like me, but enough youngsters to thwart an age discrimination suit. When the last arrive, the doors are closed, and Skip Perkinson stands on a platform to address the group.

"Thank you all for coming," he begins. "As you know, the Bishop Group has had an unfortunate event that has affected our family of employees."

Skip drones on for a painful ten minutes before getting to the point of his address. As marvelous as Skip tells us we are, we have been in effect voted off the island. HR representatives are standing by in the adjoining room to process us. We will not be allowed to return to the Bishop building, and all of our personal items will be packed up and sent to us by courier.

Mazie raises her hand. "Mr. Perkinson, I have medication in my desk. May I be allowed to go back and get it?"

Good one, Mazie. I am sure that she and Amy are trying to figure out some way to cover their tracks, horrified that some stranger will soon be rifling through the enterprise they ran out of their cubes. Relax, ladies. First, no one in HR will ever be smart enough to figure out what you were doing, and second, to avoid looking like chumps the Bishop executive team gave you two a get-out-of-jail-free card. But of course, Mazie and Amy don't know that.

Skip refuses Mazie's request and offers to have one of the HR flunkies go back to her desk and retrieve her meds while she waits to be processed. Sophie and Cindy are crying, along with several others, while we wait for our names to be called so we can enter the processing room. Frank and Moe pace at the back of the room, cell phones attached to their ears. Mazie and Amy are not crying.

Thinking for a moment, I ask Skip if it will be all right if I go out for a smoke. He says okay, and Mazie and Amy join me, as I knew they would. We travel back down the escalator and find a shady spot by the valet stand.

"What are you going to do?" Amy asks.

"Me? I'm getting a goddamn facelift and an extended stay at a fat farm. How about you?"

Mazie laughs. "We have family in New Orleans. Maybe we'll go for a fresh start there. Who knows—when God closes a door, He sometimes opens a window."

I remember my conversation with good old Buster Connelly at the airport and how he considered pipeline explosions a tragic but necessary cost of doing business. I search around in my purse, pull out a business card, and hand it to Mazie. "You might want to look this guy up," I say. "I met him at the President's Club at the Houston airport. He owns an oil company down there, and I think he may be looking for a new secretary. He's a big LSU fan, so I would brush up on my Tiger football stats. Tell him Tanzie from Tulsa sent you."

I put my cigarette out and chuckle at the thought of Buster being bilked by these two as I head back to Salon B.

When my name is called, I walk over to a small area that has been partitioned off to allow the minimum level of privacy.

Brenda, my HR representative, sits with her laptop, opens my paper file, and explains my "package." It comes to two weeks' pay—less my recent sick time, of course—and the opportunity to sign up for COBRA health benefits for a whopping $700 a month. She does her best to project real sympathy for my situation, and I am impressed with her sincerity, given that I am about her twentieth client this morning.

"Brenda," I begin. "Would it be possible to get a copy of the review I was given in March? I didn't take a copy at the time, but I want to have a one in case I need to show it to my future employer."

Brenda flips through my file and pulls out the Bishop Performance Management Report from the blue cardboard divider. "Um, let me see if there's a copy machine around here."

I watch Brenda get up and consult with an older supervisor, then disappear from view. In her absence, I take out the manila folder and place my forged pay change authorization form in the back of the file. I smile at the outstanding job I have done forging Hal's and Skip's signatures on the approval line.

"Here you go," Brenda says when she returns as she cheerfully hands me the requested report. "If you will please sign your exit agreement, Tanzie, we'll be all done."

"Brenda, I have a question," I say, looking up from the form. "I don't think my title is correct here. Last month I was given a title change to Audit Consultant. I remember signing a form, but I didn't keep a copy. There wasn't a pay increase, but Hal gave me the new title as sort of a pat on the back for a building security audit I did. Can you please check my file?"

Brenda gives me a look and then eyes the stack of ten or so other folders still needing to be processed.

"Please," I repeat. "It's really important that I give the right title on my resume."

Brenda thumbs through my file again and stops when she finds the change form. "Oh." She looks at me. "I guess this just didn't get entered into the system."

Brenda starts clicking on her laptop and then walks over to get her supervisor. I worry for a moment that the supervisor might question it, but she, too, is looking at a very long day. And so, just as I envisioned, my title change is finalized in the interest of moving the process along. Brenda crosses out and initials my exit agreement with the revised title. I shake hands with both women after I sign the amended agreement.

"I'm sure you'll find something soon, Tanzie," Brenda says.

"Thank you. I'm sure you will too, Brenda." I turn away and leave the makeshift processing station.

Five minutes later, I am in my Lexus pointed south on Highway 75 toward Houston. With any luck, I will be enjoying a late dinner at the club with Beth and Grant.

———◆———

After several months of monitoring email accounts, thanks to Baldwin's predictable password selection, and attending secret meetings via conference calls, I have compiled quite a bit of damaging evidence. Although none of it can be used in court, it could certainly prove valuable in squeezing information out of others at Bishop.

I call my old friend Bill Matheson, the Houston lawyer who has been working on the explosion settlements. "Bill, this is Tanzie Lewis. Remember me?"

"How are ya, Tanzie! I've been trying to reach you for months now. Thanks for finally calling me back. What can I do for ya?"

"I need to find out about attorney-client privilege," I begin.

"Why is that, Tanzie?"

"You have something I want, and I have something you need."

In October 2010, the *Houston Chronicle* reports that a Houston sewer contractor has admitted liability for the pipeline explosion, for not observing the "call before you dig" protocol required, and I know my time has come. I send bundles to the Justice Department, DOT enforcement, the FBI Houston District Office, and good old Dan at the *Tulsa World*.

I suddenly have a ringside seat to the biggest corporate implosion since Enron. Jury awards to victims of the explosion are predicted to set records, as the recent BP Deepwater Horizon fiasco in the Gulf of Mexico is creating a lynch mob mentality toward oil companies. Bennet's fear of margin calls and a credit squeeze were spot on.

Bad publicity makes creditors nervous, and one by one they call for margins and tighten credit limits on Bishop commodity trades. Plaintiff lawyers scream for potential damages to be placed in escrow to protect victims. In the course of two months after mailing the incriminating information, operating cash is drained, and bankruptcy rumors, once brushed off as nonsense, now look like a reality. Loyal coworkers who had built their careers at Bishop turn on each other like dogs after the same dead skunk.

Baldwin and Bennet remain loyal to each other, but both

are looking at very long, painful, and expensive litigation and criminal proceedings. Assets are frozen, and the trustees who will run Bishop on behalf of the bankers show up in Tulsa by the limo-full. The Bishop brothers themselves are no longer welcome members of Tulsa society. Their poor judgment has left Tulsa charities short-funded and hundreds of employees without jobs. Bill Matheson's fortune is going to skyrocket, only immaterially affected by the loss of a particularly friendly black Lab.

———◆———

"We received your funds transfer, Mrs. Lewis," says the fresh-faced banker. "If you sign right here, the trusts will be set up and you can be on your way."

"Thanks."

"You certainly are a generous aunt, setting up college funds for all those nieces and nephews. And the Matthew Mayhew Scholarship at SMU. Any chance you would like to be an honorary aunt to my two?"

I laugh as I get up, grab my purse, and shake his hand goodbye. "Thanks for your help on this," I say. "It's a wonderful feeling to be able to make a difference in people's lives."

CHAPTER TWENTY

I arrive for my first day at my new job in my black suit, my hair pulled back with a large barrette. It feels good to be slim again and even better to have a fresh face and neck sans wrinkles and sags. Framed photos of a fleet of coal-fired power plants hang behind my new boss's balding head. I flash a Lumineer smile as I settle into the leather chair across from his desk.

"We expect great things from you, Tanzie. A promotion after only five months on the job is impressive."

"Thanks!" I tell him. "It was so nice working for people who appreciated hard work. I'm really going to miss my old team at Bishop."

"I read a little something about your former employer in *WSJ* this morning," my new boss says. "God, what a shit-storm that turned out to be."

"I can't believe it. They were just the nicest group up there;

like family, really. I had no idea any of that was going on. I hope you don't think I'm a bad auditor."

"Not at all, hon."

"Thank you for taking a chance with me. I'm certain I can get up to speed in no time."

"Oh, I'm sure you can. Take it slow and enjoy it. Just like you know what." He leans forward and gives me a creepy wink.

I take a minute to compose myself, hoping that the disgust leaching through my pores is not visible to my new boss. Still, I feel a familiar twinge of excitement as I laugh and smile back.

"That's a stunning painting in the reception area," I tell him. "Do you know who the artist is?"

"No ma'am, but it cost a shitload of money. You can be sure of that."

"I just know I'm going to like it here," I say. "Thank you so much for this opportunity."

I get up and walk to the door, but I stop just short.

"Have you considered performing a building security audit?"

"Now that's a good idea," he says. "How soon do you think you could get going on that, hon?"

ABOUT THE AUTHOR

JOANNE FOX PHILLIPS is a graduate of the University of Texas at Austin and the director of internal audit for a midstream oil and gas company in Tulsa, Oklahoma. She is a CPA, certified internal auditor, and certified fraud examiner. This is her first attempt at writing something longer and hopefully more entertaining than an audit report. She thanks her friends, family, coworkers, and editorial team for suffering through early drafts and providing encouragement and advice throughout the process.

CPSIA information can be obtained at www.ICGtesting.com
Printed in the USA
LVOW10s0817040914

402218LV00001B/1/P